CW00860189

Santa vs Aliens

Leigh Snelson

To Josh.

Happy Christmas

Leigh Snelson

Cover artwork acknowledgements:

Elf character designed by Pikisuperstar

Alien character designed by Brgfx

All other artwork designed by Freepik

All artwork supplied by Freepik

Condition of Sale

For more information please visit:
www.leighsnelson.co.uk

Published by **Jacobson Studios**

ISBN: 9798652245184

Chapter 1

The snow settled on the rooftops. In the distance a rather croaky choir finished their attempt at Silent Night. The night was indeed silent.

The clouds occasionally parted, revealing a starry sky that reflected in the window. On the other side of this frosty glass a teenage boy with dark hair had finally accepted that the snow was melting faster than it was falling and, in all likelihood, tomorrow his school would be open as normal.

Of course, tomorrow would not be a normal day. The last day before the Christmas break was always an exciting day and as much as Frankie enjoyed the idea of staying in bed and watching TV, in truth he really didn't want to miss school.

A dim lamp lit up his small bedroom as he sat at his computer. Above him a pile of textbooks perched on the edge of a bookshelf, waiting for Frankie to be underneath, not paying attention, ready to fall onto him and get revenge for the abuse they received in his bag every day at school.

His bedsheets, covered with rockets and space stations were nearly ten years old but still looked like new. They were currently crumpled at the foot of the bed, exactly where he had left them this morning and his pillow was somewhere near the door, where he had thrown it at whoever tried to wake him.

Nobody said growing up was going to be easy and Frankie was quite prepared to sleep away the next few years and wake up when he turned eighteen.

The old Christmas movie he had been watching had finally finished and now the news glared out of the TV set that hung on the wall. A news reporter stood talking about an unusual amount of shooting stars in the sky, or flashing lights, or something. Frankie was not paying attention.

If he had been paying attention, he would have noticed that some of the stars outside were moving faster than normal. He would have also noticed that Dexter, the family dog, was spending a lot of time outside, in the snow, staring up into the night sky.

Frankie was too busy to notice any of this. The laptop was the thing that held his focus and in particular, the badly lit spaceship that he was currently walking his spaceman through.

"Over there in the shadows." Chloe's voice came through the speakers as Frankie turned and fired a laser beam into the dark corner on the control room. A console exploded and something small scuttled away into the darkness.

"Quickly, trap it." Frankie ordered.

Another character, wearing an old-fashioned space suit aimed her gun at the little green monster, she fired but missed. The creature leapt towards Frankie. A little green head, with big black eyes and two antennas instead of ears, jumped straight at him and he fell back in his chair.

A little smile crept across his face as he realised the game had actually scared him. He looked back, expecting to see his character being eaten by the alien, but instead, the creature was held in mid-air, inches from his face, unable to move and glowing blue.

"Quickly, grab its weapon and we can get out of here" Chloe ordered as her character held the alien, floating in the middle of the room.

He tapped some buttons on the keyboard and his character, wearing a spacesuit inspired by Iron Man, walked up to the creature and retrieved the device in the alien's hand.

"Nearly got it." He said as he continued to tap repeatedly on his mouse button.

"I can't hold it much longer." Chloe moaned as the tapping of her keyboard could now be heard through the speakers too.

"Got it!" He said, as he turned around to watch the creature vanish into a cloud of green dust.

"Great! Now we can complete the quest." Chloe confirmed as her spaceman, wearing the same spacesuit as the men who walked on the moon, made its way over to Frankie's. "You up for another quest?"

"I would like too but I have to help Marko with his lines one more time." Frankie insisted as he looked up at the clock next to his bed. It read seven twenty-eight. Two minutes until Marko would ring, he was always on time.

"No problem, I need to practice my guitar and put some finishing touches to my costume anyway." She said as her spaceman disappeared from the control room.

"You still haven't told me what movie character you are going as." He asked as he started logging off from the game.

"I know, you'll have to wait until tomorrow." She laughed, teasingly.

"I expect great things if you are going to beat last year's werewolf."

"I don't think you will be disappointed. Anyway, I'll let you go to Marko, he'll be mad at me if I make you late."

"Thanks, I'll see you tomorrow! Goodnight!" With that last comment the speakers dinged, and the connection was gone.

Frankie brought up a script on his computer, not that he needed it. He had been practising with Marko for weeks and he knew it word for word, he wasn't even in the play.

The moment the clock displayed seven-thirty, Frankie's phone started to chirp and the face of a Jamaican boy, with short, frizzy black hair appeared on his screen.

"Hi Marko, ready for tomorrow?" He asked.

"I was born ready!" replied Marko, confident as ever.

"Is your sister joining in tonight?" Frankie asked, readying the script.

"You mean you didn't hear about her?" Marko asked.

"No, what happened?"

"You didn't hear what happened in art class?" He asked again.

"No, tell me!"

"You mean you don't know what happened to Sophia?" Marko teased one more time.

"Just tell me!" Frankie moaned as he got bored with the constant questioning.

"Kevin spilt green paint all across the desk when he was painting a Christmas tree." Marko explained.

"That sounds about right, he is a bit clumsy." Frankie confirmed.

"Well guess who was leaning under the desk getting something out of her bag."

"It spilt onto Sophia?"

"All over her hair!" Marko said as he started laughing.

"She must have gone mental!"

"She nearly had a panic attack, she loves her blonde hair, she had to go to the toilets and wash it out." Marko continued.

"Did it work?" Frankie asked.

"Nope, and she's been in the bathroom ever since we got home so I don't think she will be practising with us tonight."

"Fair enough then, one last run-through?" Frankie asked as he found the start of the script.

"Who are you talking too?" A voice blasted in from the other side of the room and once again Frankie jumped in his seat.

"Jess! Some privacy please!" Frankie shouted at his little sister stood at the door. The small, ginger-haired girl was three and a half years younger than Frankie but in Frankie's opinion, she walked around with the confidence of a middle-aged woman.

"Is that the script for tomorrows play?" She asked as she ran across the room, over the piles of clothes and towards the laptop.

Frankie had just enough time to close the lid before she got close enough to read it.

"Yes, but it isn't for you! You'll have to wait until tomorrow." He said.

"It's going to be great though!" Marko confirmed from the phone that sat next to the laptop.

"Hi Marko!" Jess said. "I heard what happened to Sophia, I hope she is okay."

"She'll be fine, it's only green hair, she'll get over it." He confirmed.

"What do you want anyway?" Frankie scowled at his little sister.

"I am just bored and excited about tomorrow, is it as good as people say?" She asked for the millionth time tonight.

"I forgot it's your first year at middle school. You are in for a treat!" Marko's voice came out of the little phone "At the end are you going to come and get a selfie with me and the cast?"

"I can't, I don't have a mobile phone yet, Santa is bringing me one for Christmas." She replied.

"Santa? Really?" Marko asked.

"Yes, my *nine-year-old* sister has asked Santa for a mobile phone." Frankie said, reminded his friend of his younger sisters age. "Don't get your hopes up, a mobile phone is very expensive."

"I know but you had one when you were my age." She reminded him.

"Yes, but that was a long time ago, things cost a lot more these days." He fought back.

"I don't care, it's only fair, besides, I think I saw the box on mums' bed a few weeks ago."

"Well if you saw it in mums' room, then it isn't for you, all your presents are with Santa." Frankie reminded her.

"Oh yeah." She said, the disappointment visible on her face.

"Jess, you know about Santa, right?" Marko asked carefully, sensing the tone of the room.

"The jolly fat man that brings presents at Christmas? Sure." Jess replied, a hint of joy returning to her voice.

"Do you know his history?" Marko pressed.

"I think so, he lives in Lapland and has a factory at the North Pole where he makes all the gifts. He has an army of elves and reindeer that can fly. Also, he was called Saint Nicholas." She explained.

"That's right, but now there are so many people in the world that he cannot make all the gifts in his factory, although he still delivers them all." Marko continued

"So where does he make them?" She asked.

"Every year Santa makes everybody a single present, but sometimes your parents want to give you more, so they buy you gifts and send them to Santa for delivery on Christmas Eve."

"Is that why I had to give the gifts I bought Mum and Frankie to my dad, so he could give them to Santa?"

"That's right." The boy in the phone confirmed.

"Wait, you have got me a gift?" Frankie asked.

"Dad said that now I'm at middle school I had too." She explained, then stuck her tongue out at her brother.

"Every house has a place to drop off presents that only your parents know about, and the elves will come and collect them for Santa." Marko continued.

"What present have you got me?" Frankie asked again.

"And then Santa delivers the presents at Christmas." Jess said, ignoring her brother.

"Yes, but only if you have been good." Marko reminded her.

"So that mobile phone box I saw at the back of mums wardrobe could be for me?" The happiness returned to her face as she realised the phone could be for her.

"I thought you said you saw it on mums' bed?" Frankie asked.

"Maybe, or maybe I was looking for it, does it matter?" Jess started to hop around the room, excited that she might be getting a mobile phone.

"I hope you weren't looking for it, that could get you on the naughty list." Marko interrupted.

"Really?" Jess said, instantly stopping her gleeful bouncing and returning to the phone.

"I have heard about kids being put on the naughty list for less." Frankie added.

"You still have time to be good, go and ask your mum now if she has anything that she needs you to do." Marko suggested.

"Good idea!" Jess said as she jumped across the room, out of the door and down the stairs.

"That was amazing, I hope your acting is that good tomorrow in the play!" Frankie complimented.

"You know it will be and you better laugh!"

"Don't worry, I will always be there to laugh at you." Frankie chuckled to himself.

"Not laugh at me! At the jokes." The phone hissed.

"Well, I have heard them a thousand times already, but I'll try!"

"Sophia is out of the shower, I better jump in before she decides she still hasn't got all the green out. See you in the morning!" Marko's voice was already becoming distant as he ran away from his phone.

"Good Night!" Frankie shouted after him.

Outside the bedroom door, a clatter could be heard downstairs as Jess wandered around shouting to her mum and asking if there was anything she could do to help.

Frankie let out a smile which turned into a large yawn and he realised that he would need to sleep soon if he was going to have enough energy for tomorrow.

He shut down the computer and started to prepare for bed. He opened his cupboard and made sure that his outfit was complete and that his lightsabre that he received last Christmas was plugged in and charging. Tomorrow was going to be a fun day!

Chapter 2

The ground glowed white with patches of snow that remained from the previous night, but it was not enough to cancel the day's events. The school website confirmed that they were still open and reminded students that it was a fancy-dress day.

Frankie stood on the side of the road waiting for the bus with his little sister Jess. He had started to get the hang of school, after all, this was his third Christmas and he only had one more before high school. This year was different, this year he had Jess to look after and it had been a struggle so far. Stepping up and being the big brother was proving difficult.

Today was no exception. She was still fiddling with her costume and Frankie was sure that it wouldn't last the day. She was in the youngest class and they traditionally dressed up as the nativity. Wise men and shepherds dotted the streets waiting for the school bus to arrive. This was the traditional Bible story but it had received an update on who attended the birth of Jesus. Jess stood on the side of the road as proof that modern times required a modern storyteller.

She was dressed in the now infamous role of the Amazon delivery driver. She carried a large box and a pen so that Mary could sign for the package. She stood in the side of the road practising her only line in the play.

"I bring a gift from God, please sign here." Jess mumbled under her breath repeatedly, occasionally changing the tone and speed to test out different ways of saying it.

Frankie wasn't too bothered about his sister's ramblings, but he was starting to become aware of the half dozen other students who were standing around looking at her and whispering.

"Jess. You need to stop talking to yourself, people will think your strange." He warned his sister.

"I don't mind, people can think what they want." She replied as she continued playing with different voices for her role.

"Well, I don't want people talking about me." Frankie argued as he turned his back to the onlookers.

"People already think you're strange, I wouldn't worry about it." Jess laughed as she took a swipe at her big brother.

"What do you mean? People don't think I'm strange. If they do, it's only because of you!" Frankie replied, getting closer so Jess didn't have to shout.

"Well, you're the one dressed as a Star Wars; they are looking and laughing at you too." Jess explained as she looked at him and chuckled at his outfit.

"I'm a Jedi! Our class theme is movies." Frankie said, waving his lightsabre in front of his sister's face.

"Yeah, well, it's strange."

She did have a point. There was a strong divide in school between those who took dress up day seriously and those who just wanted to not wear the school uniform for a day.

Frankie took it very seriously and he couldn't wait to show off his costume to his friends and also check out their creations. They had been planning this since

October and now, finally, the day had arrived, as did the bus.

It was the oldest, most rust-covered vehicle anyone had ever seen and somehow it managed to get over thirty children to school and back every day. Frankie understood that no bus company would use their best buses for school, but the company could have at least installed working seatbelts.

He started to climb up through the open door before stopping and realising that Jess needed help with the huge parcel that she was carrying. It was almost bigger than her and would take up an entire seat to itself.

He grabbed it off his struggling sister and held it over his head as he looked for a seat.

"What's in the box?" A voice came from the back of the bus.

"Is that my parcel?" Another boy shouted up.

"Ignore them." Frankie said as he put the box on the seat next to his sister and then sat behind her.

"Hey Frankie. Nice dressing gown. Did you forget to get dressed this morning?" The same boy shouted down the bus.

He was about to turn around and shout something back but he couldn't think of anything clever enough. Frankie has never been very good with banter. It wasn't a dressing gown, it was a Jedi cloak, but they wouldn't understand and it wasn't worth the effort trying to explain.

The same boys had been teasing Frankie every day on the bus. They were a year older and would be moving on to high school in the summer, then they would understand what it was like to get picked on by older boys. This thought comforted him.

"Stand up for yourself. Why don't you ever say anything?" Jess asked as she turned around in her seat.

"It's not worth it. I actually feel sorry for them, they don't have many friends because they make fun of everyone they meet." Frankie explained.

"Yeah, well it wouldn't hurt you to stand up for yourself every once and a while." Jess snapped and turned back to face the front of the bus.

The ride was uneventful, just like every other day and Frankie sat with his head pressed up against the glass as he watched the snow-covered ground whiz past the window.

He lived in a small village in the middle of nowhere while his friends lived much closer to school. They walked to school together but Frankie had to endure this twenty-minute ride every morning. Boring!

Every couple of minutes new people would get on and Frankie could admire the costumes and the effort that people put in. Most were wearing ugly Christmas jumpers with terrible designs on them. There was one kid who had a picture of Jesus with the tag line 'Birthday Boy' and a balloon in his hand.

Then the twins got on. These two always went all out, trying to compete with each other. They wore quite elaborate Pharaoh and Roman emperor outfits. Their class theme was obviously ancient characters.

After a few more stops Jess's friend joined the bus. She lived close enough that she could walk to school, but her parents argued she was too young so she was given a bus pass.

Nine years old was old enough to walk the half a mile to school in Frankie's opinion. How many minutes had this extra stop added to the journey this year? Frankie didn't like to think about the hours lost.

Jess's friend was dressed up as a Christmas present and struggled to climb on board. Clearly, her parents didn't think of the practicalities of wearing a giant box all day at school. Every year there were always a couple of students who make the mistake of wearing something impractical. The boy who came dressed as an Egyptian mummy, only to have the toilet roll slowly unroll itself throughout the day, fortunately, he had clothes on underneath.

Last year, four girls, Faith, Amy, Issie and Lottie all decided to each wear a large cardboard letter of their name. It was only when they saw the photos later, that they realised they spelt out 'FAIL' when they stood next to each other.

Jess's friend won't make the same mistake next year, especially as she sat down and disappeared inside the gift-wrapped box. Just a box with legs now sat opposite.

Finally, the bus came to a stop and the doors opened. Frankie began to stand up but waited as the stampeding elephants from the back of the bus barged their way through. For kids who claimed to hate school, they were always in a hurry to get off the bus.

Jess ran away to her friends and Frankie made the long walk over to the bike racks where he knew his friends would be waiting.

He could hear the commotion before he could see what was happening. As he turned the corner it all became clear.

First, he saw Sophia. A bright green ball gown decorated with white wool, tinsel and a floppy hat to match. She was playing Mrs Claus in the school play but right now her head was buried in her phone adjusting a photo of herself, applying filters, smoothing wrinkles and changing the lighting. Frankie didn't understand why she did any of this, but it's what kept her busy.

"Hi Sophia!" He said as he approached.

Holding up a finger to ask Frankie to wait while she tapped on the phone a few more times before finally turning it off and looking at him.

"Hi!" She said in her usual, upbeat mood.

"I like your costume, Mrs Claus?" Frankie asked.

"Thanks, and luckily the hat covers my hair, it still has a green tint to it." Sophia said as she tucked away a stray curl of greenish blonde hair.

"Yeah, I heard about what happened yesterday. Don't worry, you can't tell." Frankie assured her.

"I like your costume! You're one of those star men, right?" Sophia asked.

"I'm a Jedi, and wow! You are worse than my sister!" Frankie quipped back.

"Sorry, you know I'm not into all that stuff but I do like how plush and soft your dressing gown is, what material is it?" She didn't give Frankie any warning before turning him around and inspecting the label.

"Careful, it's my dad's." Frankie protested but it was no good, he just had to put up with it.

"Nice Lightsabre!" Frankie heard from across the yard. It was Marko, he was wearing a green Santa outfit that matched his sisters and quickly he walked over and slapped his sister's hands away from Frankie's collar.

"You need to learn boundaries." Marko said to his sister.

"I just wondered if it was made of cashmere, it isn't." Sophia argued back.

"It's fine" Frankie said as he pulled in his collar to return it to its normal place. "You guys both look good, I can't wait for the show!"

Marko and Sophia were often called twins. They shared the same birthday, lived in the same house and lived with the same parents. Standing next to each other you wouldn't know all this. Sophia was a pretty girl with long blonde hair, pale skin and blue eyes, short and obsessed with her looks. Her brother, Marko, was much taller, very athletic, had brown eyes, dark curly hair and was from Jamaican origins, giving him the darkest skin Frankie had ever seen.

Their parents had got married when they were both very young. Sophia, unfortunately, lost her mum during childbirth and was raised by her dad. Marko never knew who his dad was either, a hurricane took his life when Marko was only a baby. Marko and his mum moved away from Jamaica soon after and his mum found Sophia's dad, they were still only babies at the time, barely a year old. The fact that they share the same birthday is a perfect coincidence.

Together they captained the school sports teams, ran the school council and had taken the lead roles in every play that Frankie could remember. They had been busy for weeks trying to learn their lines and choosing their outfits. The green costumes for Santa and Mrs Claus was a twist on the traditional red thanks to the school council's energy-saving concerns, they were green for the environment, a detail Sophia mentioned all the time.

The commotion in the yard started to grow and for once it wasn't surrounding either of these two. Instead, a group of people crowded around a small girl who was busy trying to lock up her bike and really didn't like the attention. It was Chloe.

This had been the moment Frankie had been waiting for. Chloe had been promising big things with her costume this year. Months ago, they were trying to think of ideas, Frankie mentioned that he could use his dads dressing gown as a Jedi costume, Chloe had some crazy idea that she started to design, but she had kept it a secret, somehow, until now.

The crowd started to part, revealing Chloe in her outfit. Frankie's jaw dropped! She must have been working on it night and day. Although it was only made from cardboard, the craftsmanship was incredible. There, in the middle of the crowd stood a miniature version of Iron Man.

"Chloe! That's impossible. How did you, when did you…" Frankie found himself unable to finish sentences, instead, he stood there in utter disbelief at the sight in front of him.

The cardboard robot started to make its way towards him and then, without warning, the helmet flipped up and revealed the grinning face of Chloe.

"I know! It's turned out better than I could have expected!"

"How long did it take to make all this!?" The amazement was obvious in Frankie's voice, and his wide eyes indicated his delight.

"Hold on, let me show you everything!" Chloe pulled the facemask down and returned it over her face. "I use rubber bands and strings running down the arms to these buttons."

She held up her hands that were wrapped in cardboard gloves. In the middle were a set of buttons and with her middle finger, she pressed the biggest one. Once again her faceplate sprung up above her head.

"That's so cool." Frankie remarked.

"It also does this." She said as she twisted her wrist. Lights, dotted around the suit, turned on and started to glow.

"Awesome." Frankie admired.

"I know, and check these out." She pressed the buttons in the middle of each hand and the cardboard shoulder panels popped up revealing foam bullets ready to be fired.

"Hey, they are from the Nerf gun I got you for your birthday!" Frankie objected. "Do they work?"

"Of course!" Chloe turned to face Marko who was now chatting with another cast member on the other side of the courtyard. She twitched her left hand and a rocket flew from her shoulder, across the small distance between her and Marko and, just as he was about to say something, the little plastic missile flew straight into his open mouth.

"Good shot!" Sophia said as she started to laugh at her brother who was now choking on a foam dart.

Instantly the whole yard erupted with laughter at the precise shot. Marko spat out the bullet and strode over to Chloe holding it out for her to take back.

"I believe this is yours!"

"Erm, you can keep it." She said as she looked at the dart, wet from Marko's mouth, sitting in his hand.

"You didn't say you could aim like that! Is it laser-guided or something?" Marko asked, impressed at the accuracy of the suit.

"It was just luck this time." Chloe admitted as she twisted her wrist and the shoulder pads returned to their original positions, hiding the darts underneath the cardboard.

"You have to give me the designs, I need to make one for myself!" Frankie insisted.

"We'll see, let's get inside first, the bell is about to go." Chloe grinned and once again put the mask back on. "I am Cardboard Woman!"

"Tell Mrs Smith that Sophia and I are going straight to the hall for last-minute rehearsals." Marko shouted as he joined his sister who had already started to head towards the entrance to the large hall.

"Will do!" Frankie shouted back as he turned and walked with Chloe over to the main school entrance.

The rest of the crowd also started to head towards the doors only to find a group of teachers out collecting for charity. The deal was simple, you don't have to wear the school uniform but you have to make a small donation to charity.

Frankie already had his coins ready to put on the collection plate and he watched as his sister, further up in the queue, made her donation with her friends.

He also noticed that before him were the same older boys from the bus ride and they were trying their hardest not to give over their money.

"It's nice weather today, clear skies and not too cold." The first boy said to Mr Brown who was holding the collection plate. Mr Brown was the school's sports teacher and he knew the boys very well.

"Yes, it is, it's going to be a good day." He replied, shaking the plate to get the boys attention.

"I am looking forward to the performances today. I hear Marko is going to give a good show as Santa." The boy continued, ignoring the plate that was thrust at him.

"Well, he has been working hard on it, he should be entertaining." Mr Brown replied, shaking the plate with even more vigour.

"And I love your reindeer outfit." The boy continued, drawing attention to the antlers that stuck out of Mr Browns head.

"Actually, it's a moose, because I am from Canada." Mr Brown corrected.

"A moose? That's awesome! Merry Christmas!" The boy finished, walking away from the antler topped teacher.

"Jonny, you still need to pay." Mr Brown reminded him as he started to leave.

"Oh yeah, I nearly forgot." Jonny said as he reluctantly dug into his pockets and found the coin he was looking for.

"Of course you did." Mr Brown said, knowingly. He had seen it all before. Jonny wouldn't be the first, nor the last student to think he was smarter than Mr Brown.

"Merry Christmas." Jonny said again, putting his money on the plate and walking away making room for his friend behind him.

"Happy Holidays." Mr Brown said once again as he thrust the plate towards the next boy.

"Mr Brown, do they celebrate Christmas in Canada?" Jonny suddenly shouted back. This caused Mr Brown to take his attention away from the plate and back to Jonny who was now standing on top of the steps into the school.

"Yes, of course. In fact, where I come from there are already huge piles of snow, much better than this little sprinkle we get around here." He explained, completely focused on Jonny.

This moment was clearly planned as Jonny's friend saw his chance and picked up three of the coins from the plate without the teacher noticing. Jonny was doing an excellent job of distracting Mr Brown. He pocketed one of the coins, slid one to his friend behind him and held the final coin above the plate, then he let out a little cough to get the teachers attention.

"Merry Christmas." The new boy said as he put the stolen coin back onto the plate, making sure to be noticed.

"And Merry Christmas from me too." The boy behind interrupted and put the other stolen coin back on the plate.

"Merry Christmas boys, and thank you for your generosity." Mr Brown said, unaware of the scam they had just pulled. He stood smiling at them as they wandered off to join Jonny again.

Frankie saw the boy hand Jonny his original coin and the three of them all ran into school as quickly as they could.

"Did you see that?" Frankie asked Chloe, shocked at the performance that he had just witnessed

"I can't see anything in this mask." Chloe replied. "What happened?"

"Jonny and the other bullies just got in without giving to charity." Frankie explained. "It's just not in the spirit of Christmas."

"Say something then." Chloe urged.

"Nah, no-one will listen to me. Besides, they won't always get away with it, one day they will get caught out." Frankie assured himself.

"Merry Christmas." Frankie said as he put his coin on the plate.

"Merry Christmas Frankie, and who is this?" Mr Brown's attention turned to the cardboard clad figure.

Once again, the mask slid up over Chloe's head to reveal her face.

"Hi!" Chloe said, dropping her money on the plate.

"Chloe, that is very impressive." Mr Brown praised.

"Thank you. It took ages to make."

"I bet it did. Well done!" The teacher said, admiring the craftwork that had gone into the costume.

"We better get inside. If the cardboard gets too cold the glue might start breaking." Chloe explained as she rushed Frankie up the steps and into the warm school building.

Chapter 3

Inside, school was business as usual. Frankie and Chloe made their way down the corridor to the classroom where Kevin would be waiting for them. He usually got dropped off at school early by his dad.

Frankie opened the door to class 3B and saw his friend. Sitting in his usual seat he wore a red jumper, beige trousers and a sash that contained little pockets to hide things in.

"You're the kid from Home Alone!" Frankie said as he walked into the classroom, immediately recognising the costume. Kevin also happened to look like the boy from the movie and share the same name.

"And you're a Jedi. Is that the lightsabre you got last year for Christmas?" Kevin asked.

"Yep, and I borrowed my dad's dressing gown but don't tell anyone." He explained. "Have you seen Chloe yet?"

"No, but I am expecting that she has gone over the top, as usual, you know what she is…" He was cut off as his eyes caught the sight of the cardboard robot that entered the classroom.

"Yes, that is Chloe." Frankie confirmed as he saw Kevin's jaw drop and eyes widen.

"That's amazing!"

"Wait until you see what it can do!" Frankie said as he gestured for Chloe to join them on the table.

"Hold on, it's not easy to sit down in this thing." She said as she struggled to sit behind her desk.

"That is so cool!" Kevin stated as he reached out to touch the face mask. His hand was inches away when it popped open and his outstretched finger nearly poked Chloe in the eye.

"Do you mind!" she said. "Don't make me launch the rockets."

"It has rockets?" Kevin asked as he pulled his hand away.

Chloe made an arm movement and the little compartments on her shoulders popped up to reveal nerf guns ready and loaded.

"Cool!" Kevin said as more amazement grew over his face. "Do they work?"

Without hesitation, Chloe twitched her finger and a foam bullet shot out from her shoulder and hit Frankie directly between the eyes. A perfect shot.

"Hey! What did I do?" Frankie moaned as he picked up the little missile and threw it back at the cardboard superhero.

"So, who are you?" Chloe asked Kevin as she picked up the foam bullet and tucked it away for later.

"I'm the kid from Home Alone." Kevin replied, standing up and twirling so that she could see the knitted red jumper, an orange t-shirt underneath and denim trousers. He also wore a leather belt over his shoulder that had six pockets stuck to it.

"Nice sash, did you win a beauty contest?" Frankie joked at the leather band.

"It's called a bandolier, my dad uses it when he goes hunting, it's great to store stuff in." Kevin explained. "I know it wasn't part of the movie but I think it completes the look."

"Home Alone? I haven't seen that one." Chloe admitted as she flashed her costume lights on and off.

"What! It's possibly the best movie ever made!" Kevin said as he started to rise out of his chair and fiddle with the pockets on his bandolier.

"Yeah, it's the ultimate Christmas movie about a kid who gets left behind." Frankie backed Kevin up. "I can't believe you haven't seen it."

"What's so special about being alone at Christmas?" She asked.

"It's not about being alone, it's about how a kid sets traps in his house to catch criminals." Kevin explained as he emptied several of his pockets to reveal an assortment of traps and toys.

"It's a good movie." Frankie added. "You really should watch it, I think you, out of all of us, would love it."

"A movie about setting traps. What kind of traps?" Chloe asked.

"Well." Kevin spread out the contents of his satchel. "You can drop marbles on the floor so that people slip on them, tie tripwire to the edge of door frames or use radios to make it sound like you're somewhere else."

"Is that your dad's fishing wire?" Frankie asked as he picked up the thin spool of wire on the desk. The moment he touched it the wire began to uncurl itself from around the spindle and fall to the floor. Frankie frantically started to roll it up, but it kept spreading, and he was sure someone would genuinely trip on it if he wasn't quick.

"It sure is." Kevin said as he watched Frankie struggle with the thin wire, like he was wrestling with a snake.

"Okay, trip wire I understand." Chloe said, looking at Frankie but refusing to help as he now dropped the wire and it exploded on the floor. "What else?"

"There is slime that can be used to make handles slippery and a trusty swiss army knife because you never know!"

"Wait! You brought a knife to school?" She asked, quite alarmed at the idea.

"Yeah right, my parents won't trust me with a real knife, this is made of plastic from when I was a kid." He held out the toy knife to confirm it was no danger.

"It sounds like a bit of a goofy movie." Chloe said as she reached down and inspected a toy dart gun that was still on the desk.

"You need to watch it. Kevin isn't doing it justice." Frankie said, finally getting the fishing line back in order and handing it back to Kevin who immediately dropped it and caused it to unravel again.

"You guys are just accidents waiting to happen." Chloe said, embarrassed at the clumsiness. She reached up and slid her facemask back into place to hide her shame.

"Come on! I just fixed that!" Frankie moaned as they watched the spool roll over to the door where it was stopped by a strange boot.

"Good morning class." Mrs Smith said as she walked into the classroom just as the bell rang. Everyone's eyes darted across the room as they all got up and stood behind their chairs in the usual morning ritual.

"Good Morning Mrs Smith." The class rang out in unison, then everyone sat down, everyone except Chloe who struggled to bend in her suit. Once she had figured it out and found her seat she immediately threw her hand up in the air to get the teachers attention.

"Yes, erm, Chloe I assume?" Mrs Smith stuttered as she stared at the cardboard covered girl.

Chloe triggered the elastic bands again and her mask sprung up above her head. This time, however, it didn't stop. It flew across the room as people ducked out of its way. It collided with the star on the top of the class tree, knocked it off and replaced it.

"Good morning, I love your costume!" Chloe complimented, unaware that her mask had just flown across the room.

"Thank you, Chloe. What does everyone think?" Mrs Smith stood at the front of the class and spun around to show off her outfit. If anyone had walked into the room at that moment they would be sure they were meeting Johnny Depp as Mrs Smith was dressed exactly like the pirate from the movie. It was a fantastic costume and everyone was in awe at the attention to detail.

"It looks like the real thing!" Chloe replied as she reached above her head for the faceplate but returned empty-handed. She turned and looked at Frankie who gestured to the back of the classroom where, instead of a star, the faceplate of the famous Iron Man topped the tree.

"Thank you." Mrs Smith replied. "I know you are all excited about today, but first we need to head to the hall where there is the usual nativity from Mrs Wilsons class, then we'll come back here and vote on the best costume. Let's get going!"

The room stood up and started to make their way over to the hall. Nobody looked forward to this part of the day. They had performed this same nativity two years ago but it was a ritual, so everyone just went along with it.

"You are totally going to win the best costume!" Kevin said to Chloe as they got up and made their way down the corridor to the hall.

"Thanks, but how am I going to get my mask back from the top of the tree?" Chloe asked as she looked back towards the classroom.

"I could try and nudge it with my lightsabre." Frankie offered as he pressed a button and the plastic stick started to glow green.

"Or I could capture it with some string and fishing hooks." Kevin suggested as he looked in his sash and pulled out a piece of string of unknown length.

"All good suggestions but I think I'll just ask Mrs Smith." Chloe said as she looked at the two boys who were swinging plastic lightsabres and fishing line around. "You two will probably pull the tree down before the mask falls off."

"Hey, we aren't that clumsy!" Frankie objected, just as Kevin somehow managed to tie his own hands together with the string.

"Erm, a little help." He said as he held out his hands that were now bound together.

"Really?" Chloe argued as she gestured to the now helpless boy.

"Okay, maybe Kevin is." Frankie laughed as he started to unravel his friend.

"Do we have to go and see the nativity." A voice cried down the corridor. "We see it every year."

"Look at them." Kevin pointed to a group of girls ahead of them who were stood around moaning.

"I know! Would they rather be doing boring maths instead?" Frankie asked. "It might be boring but at least it's different."

"Hey, I wouldn't mind doing some extra maths." Chloe interrupted.

"Maybe you need it, then your costume wouldn't fall apart and fly across the room!" Frankie joked.

The shoulder compartments jumped up on Chloe's outfit again and she pointed them at Frankie.

"Don't make me shoot you again!" She threatened.

"I would like to see you try!" Frankie held out the lightsabre ready to bat away the oncoming threat.

"Oh no!" Kevin blurted out. "The slime, it's leaking and has gone everywhere!"

A wet stain could be seen seeping out of one of the pockets across Kevin's chest as slime started to drip out and onto the floor.

There were little puddles of green ooze leading back to their classroom. A small elf walked towards them and hadn't noticed the wet floor, she slipped, shifting left then right before finally catching herself and continuing down the corridor, looking back and wondering what had just caused her to lose her balance.

"Come on, lets clean you up." Frankie suggested as he pointed towards the toilets.

"I'll save you guys some seats." Chloe shouted after them as they disappeared into the boy's room.

Inside, murmurings of boys that were up-to-no-good could be heard. It was Jonny and the boys from the bus, and they were doing something near the sink.

"You two! Don't you dare tell anyone what we are doing in here!" The tallest, Jonny, said to Frankie and Kevin as they entered.

"What *are* you doing in here?" Kevin asked as he tried to see what was going on in the sink.

"Nothing to do with you!" One of the other boys said as he stepped in front and blocked the view.

Frankie could just make out the remains of a packet on the counter. They were filling water balloons. All three of them had pockets bulging as they filled the final one and stuffed it up inside Jonny's sleeve.

"You saw nothing." Jonny threatened as they turned and started to leave the bathroom.

"We saw nothing." Frankie and Kevin repeated as the boys walked past, they tried to avoid eye contact as they walked over to the sink. Kevin had already taken the sash off and started to open the pocket where the slime was leaking out.

"Remember! You saw nothing!" Jonny turned and scowled as the other two boys ran out of the door, "If anyone finds out it was us, we'll be coming for you!"

Then Jonny turned to leave the bathroom, not realising he was stood in a large puddle of slime. His legs were suddenly above his head as he landed with a thud on his back. His arms stretched out trying to grab something, anything, but the only thing he achieved was letting go of the water balloon that flew out of his sleeve, up in the air and back down, landing on his face, exploding, sending water everywhere.

Laughter erupted from Frankie and Kevin as they tried and failed to hold it back.

His face and hair were soaked but Jonny quickly got back up to his feet, grabbed a paper towel from the dispenser and stared angrily at Frankie.

"What is going on in here!" Mr Brown's voice suddenly rang out through the bathroom.

"Nothing sir." Jonny said as he turned away to hide the water balloons in his pockets.

"I don't know what is going on but you boys need to tidy yourselves up and get to the hall now, the nativity is about to start!"

"On my way." Jonny said and scuttled away to catch up with his friends. Mr Brown followed them, sensing that they might be up to something.

As the door slowly shut Frankie and Kevin blurted out in laughter one more time.

"I don't know why I am laughing, nothing ever goes right for me!" Kevin said as he started to rinse the pocket of slime.

"No, I suppose it doesn't." Frankie agreed as he started to gather paper towels and soak up the puddles of slime on the floor. "But it's always fun to be around you and witness the chaos."

"Thanks!" Kevin replied. "I just hope that Chloe managed to save us good seats!"

"I am waiting to see what Sophia does to you after yesterday." Frankie said as he dabbed up the rest of the puddle.

"It wasn't my fault; the paint was too close to the edge of the table." Kevin tried to defend his actions.

"Hey, I wasn't there, but you ruined Sophia's hair for Christmas." Frankie reminded, making Kevin feel bad.

"Do you think she will forgive me?" He asked as he started to dry his top with paper towels.

"I guess she might, but you might want to rethink the whole 'asking her on a date' thing for a while."

"Yeah, I suppose you are right. She'll never say yes now." Kevin's tone was suddenly down as he realised, he might have lost his chance with the girl he was obsessed with.

"Come on, let's go watch this boring play." Frankie said as he pulled his friends arm out of the bathroom and towards the hall.

Moments later they found their seats at the front of the hall where Chloe was waiting. The room went dark and the show began.

It was the same show that Frankie had seen twice already, and he could still remember all the lines. When his class did it, he played the front of the donkey and Kevin was the rear. The two boys didn't know each other back then but they soon became lifelong friends.

The idea of the donkey's back legs talking was always a disturbing sight, but everyone had to say something, had to learn a line, it was the rules, even if you were the rear of a donkey.

"I bring a gift from God, please sign here." Jess said her line perfectly and the rest of the play went quickly. There was only one issue, a young boy dressed as a penguin tripped on his flippers but the blood was quickly mopped up and everything went back to normal. The child, dressed as the barn door forgot to open until it was too late and smacked Joseph in the face, while Mary dropped the baby Jesus off the stage. Otherwise, it was a good show.

The lights went down after the class took their bow and then screaming filled the hall. It was terrifying as children's high-pitched yells filled the room.

As the lights returned the cause was obvious. The stage and all the cast were soaked, and the remains of water balloons were visible, especially as one of the penguins was pulling the red plastic out of his teeth.

A commotion came across the hall as the cast slipped and fell as they tried to quickly escape the stage. Finally, the curtain came down to hide the destruction. Then it went silent as an angry Mr Brown walked across the stage and took the microphone.

"Whoever that was! I expect a full, written apology on my desk by the end of the day otherwise don't expect to return in the new year!" He shouted into the microphone.

Frankie glanced over his shoulder and saw Jonny and his friends trying to hold back their laughter and keep a straight face.

"Now we have a performance from this year's drama class titled 'Is Santa Coming To Town?' Please give them a round of applause."

Mr Brown exited stage right and the curtain opened to reveal Marko and Sophia in the spotlight and ready to speak their lines.

Frankie new most of the words by now. He had helped Marko read through them many times in recent weeks and he knew the script better than anyone else. He couldn't match Marko's showmanship, however.

It was a great performance, the jokes were funny and everyone laughed at the right points, although the biggest laugh came as the extras, dressed as reindeers tried to pull Marko and Sophia across the stage on their sleigh. They couldn't manage it so Marko, dressed as Santa had to get out and push.

"It wasn't like this in rehearsal." Sophia explained to the crowd.

"You weren't wearing half a ton of makeup in rehearsal!" Marko quipped as he pushed his sister across the stage.

Towards the end Marko did go off script again when they were looking at a swamp covered in used wrapping paper.

"Why can't people just recycle." Sophia said as she gestured into the painting of a swamp that was covered in tinsel and ribbon.

"I know! This place has got more mould that your hair!" Marko joked as he pulled Sophia's hat off and revealed her green hair to the room.

Instantly he regretted it. As the crowd around him laughed, Sophia stared at him and he knew she would get her own back.

The curtain came down and the whole theatre stood up with a standing ovation. Students from lower years rushed the stage to get pictures with the cast as Frankie, Kevin and Chloe got up and returned to class.

"Look at Marko, he is a born superstar." Chloe pointed to the stage as Marko held two of the younger students above his head in a superman pose for the camera.

"Yes, he might be superman, but Sophia is still going to kill him later!" Frankie reminded them.

Chapter 4

"Okay class. Everybody take your seats." Mrs Smith instructed as everyone returned to the classroom.

"That was a great performance." Frankie congratulated Marko as they walked into the classroom together.

"Everybody, let's put our hands together one more time for the stars of the show, Marko and Sophia." Mrs Smith said as she started to clap, inviting everyone else along with her.

"Thank you!" Marko said, taking a stand at the front of the class. "Of course we had a great cast and fantastic backstage team, and I am just amazed that Sophia put her phone down long enough to learn her lines."

"Hey!" Sophia said as she put away her phone that she had been staring into, using it as a mirror to hide any stray green hairs. "I am just amazed that you could get your big ego through the door!"

"If everyone can cast their votes for the best costume then we can all head outside for the school photo." Mrs Smith said, interrupting the two arguing twins and handing them piles of voting slips to hand out.

"I know who I'm going to vote for!" Frankie said as he looked passed Chloe and at the tree where the mask still sat.

"Come on guys. We all know who we're voting for!" Marko said as he quickly wrote a name down on the paper and handed back his voting slip to Mrs Smith.

"You've got this!" Frankie whispered the Chloe as pieces of paper were passed back to the front for Mrs Smith to count.

"I'm sorry about yesterday." Kevin said to Sophia as she handed him a voting slip.

"Don't mention it, I've already thought of how I am going to get you back." Sophia cackled as she walked past and took her seat behind him.

He looked helplessly at Frankie, trying to request help but he was too busy talking to Chloe to notice, so he turned back to Sophia.

"I really am sorry." He repeated.

"I know you are. Don't worry about it." She said politely but grinned menacingly back at him.

"Here we go." Marko said as he started to drum on the desk and get everyone worked up. As more people started to join in Marko watched Mrs Smith for his cue.

After a few moments counting the results were in and Mrs Smith gave Marko a nod.

"Five…" Marko started.

"Four…" the rest of the class joined in the count down.

"Three… Two… One…" The whole class watched as Mrs Smith stood up.

"This year's winner of the Christmas outfit competition is… Chloe!" She said, clapping her hands.

Frankie grabbed Chloe and lifted her to her feet to take in the applause.

"Thank you!" Chloe said, embarrassed by the moment.

"Show us what you can do!" Marko shouted above the clapping.

Chloe stood there, pressed the buttons on her hand and once again her cardboard shoulders popped up revealing her dart guns. She twisted and fired foam darts across the class, hitting some people and landing one in the class fish tank. Then she twisted her wrist again and the lights around the suit lit up and glowed briefly, oohs and ahhs came from the class before sparks started to appear from the middle of the suit.

"Cool... oh no!" Frankie said as he first saw the light show and then the sparks.

"I don't remember Iron Man being on fire in the movies?" Sophia asked innocently. "It's a great special effect though."

"It's not a special effect." Kevin said as he reached for his water bottle and threw it to Frankie who sprayed the small flames that were coming out of the suit.

Chloe hadn't noticed any of this but as she saw Frankie catch the bottle, she looked down and saw the flames herself. Immediately she started to tear the cardboard suit off, rubber bands and string flung everywhere. Throwing the cardboard onto the floor she stamped on the wet cinders until the flames were out.

"Are you okay?" Mrs Smith asked as she ran over to Chloe.

"Yes, I'm fine, that was nothing compared to last year when I nearly hung myself with Spider man's webbing." Chloe said calmly. "Frankie, add that to the list, another invention up in flames, literally."

"Only three fires and two electric shocks this year!" Frankie commented. "Your inventions are getting better!"

"I knew it was always a possibility that's why I wore this jumper underneath." Chloe said as she pointed out the jumper which read 'I'm not short, I'm an elf.'

"I think it's time we head outside for some fresh air." Mrs Smith suggested. "It's time for the school photograph anyway."

"Photograph!" Sophia perked up. "How do I look?"

"Great!" Kevin replied.

"You would think that, everyone knows you like me." Sophia said as she threw her head back dramatically and laughed causing Kevin to go as red as his jumper.

"Oh, that's brutal." Marko laughed.

"Told you I would get my own back." She whispered to Kevin as she got out of her seat. "And that's just the start. Mwahahaha."

Kevin watched as Sophia walked away, laughing to herself. Frankie hopped over the seats to join him, his face red, his embarrassment maxed out.

"I have a bad feeling about this." He said to Frankie who pulled him to his feet.

"Don't worry, she'll forget by the time Christmas is over." Frankie tried to comfort as they caught up with the girls.

"Are you not wearing your costume to the photograph?" Sophia asked Chloe.

"No, I don't think so." Chloe said as she looked back at the crumpled pile on the floor.

"Oh well, it was great special effects, it looked like a real fire!" Sophia commented, no hint of irony in her voice. "You're going to have to show me how you do that!"

"Yeah, I'll show you sometime." Chloe rolled her eyes at Marko, Kevin and Frankie who were trying their hardest not to laugh.

"Maybe your right, maybe she will forget." Kevin whispered to Frankie.

"Sophia, I think Kevin has found your marbles." Frankie said as he pushed his friend forward towards her.

"I haven't lost any marbles." Sophia replied.

"Are you sure?" Marko jumped into the conversation, never wanting to miss an opportunity to make fun of his ditsy sister.

"Ignore them." Kevin said. "Let's go and get our photos taken."

The school wasn't very big, but it still required everyone to line up on the playground to get a whole school photograph. There was a small outside seating area with benches and tables where people would normally eat their lunch.

Everyone knew the routine for photographs now, there seemed to be a new photo every couple of weeks. The youngest year kneeled at the front, this was where Jess was, with the next year stood behind them.

Frankie's year then moved the benches together and stood on them while Jonny's year, the oldest, stood on the tables.

It took a bit of sorting but soon everyone was in position and staring back at Mr Price, Jess's teacher who also acted as the school photographer.

"Is everyone ready?" Mr Price shouted from across the yard. He held up his hand and stared through the viewfinder of the camera, making sure that everyone was in the frame. This was all normal activity, then he stood up, took a step back and stared up into the sky. This was not normal.

The flash on the camera went off but Mr Price didn't move, he just continued to stare over the crowd of students and high into the sky.

Murmurings of impatience grew as people started to fidget and wonder what was going on. Then a scream from Sophia caught everyone's attention.

She was staring behind everyone, at whatever Mr Price had seen. Everyone quickly turned their heads, following Sophia's gaze, to see whatever was so terrifying.

The sky was blue and clear, no clouds or birds, just a few dozen flying saucers, silver, round and spinning overhead, slowly moving over the town.

That was it. The whole school erupted into screams as everyone reacted to the crazy vision in the sky. Some people, like Sophia, froze in place, staring up at the metal circles that hung in the sky. Others, like Marko, were trying to get everybody to move. He was pulling on his sisters' hand, trying to get her back inside the building along with everyone else.

Kevin was the kind of person who didn't know what to do so he just stumbled around trying to make sense of the situation. Running around in circles, looking for someone to tell him what to do.

Chloe immediately reached for her phone to start recording and documenting everything.

This left Frankie to go and ask the teacher what they should do. Not that any of them had a clue, this had never been a situation they had trained for.

"Everybody back inside!" Mrs Smith suddenly shouted at the top of her voice.

Nobody needed telling twice. Everyone ran for the doors, down the corridors and into their appropriate classrooms. In all the commotion Frankie caught sight of Jess who was in tears, sitting on the floor, holding her legs tight. He leaned down and stroked her head as she looked up at him.

"Don't worry." Frankie said in his calmest voice. "Go back to class and let the grownups deal with it."

Jess took one look at Frankie and more tears appeared.

"Jess, do you want to stay with Frankie?" Mrs Smith asked as she saw the situation and walked over.

Jess nodded and hugged her older brother tight.

"Come on then you two. Let's get inside."

Moments later everyone was in the classroom and Mrs Smith was closing the blinds on the windows so that nobody could see out.

"Did you see that?" Marko asked as he looked for someone to confirm what was happening.

"I know! What do you think they are?" Kevin asked.

"My best guess is that they are an experimental aircraft from another country, my bet is the Australians, they have been very quiet recently." Chloe suggested.

"What? Australians are from another planet? I always thought they came from Earth?" Sophia asked.

"No, that's not what I meant, never mind." Chloe replied, giving up trying to make her point.

"What are you talking about? Australians? They are clearly UFO's, that means aliens!" Marko exclaimed excitedly and at the mention of the word *aliens*, Jess started to cry on Frankie's shoulder again.

"Marko, can you be a bit more sensitive." He asked as he tried to comfort his little sister.

"Sorry. What do you think the A-L-I-E-N-S want?" Marko spelt out.

Jess let out another sob.

"Dude! She's my sister, not a dog, she can spell!" Frankie moaned.

"Alan? Who's Alan?" Sophia asked.

"Why do you do that?" Marko turned and asked his sister. "We all know you can spell, why do you pretend to be a dizzy blonde?"

Before she could answer Chloe thrust her phone between everyone so they could all see.

"Check this out!"

It was a live broadcast from someone at the pyramids in Egypt. The video was titled 'Our Great Adventure' and was clearly someone's livestream of their holiday. Now it was the number one trending video on the internet.

On the screen flying metal aircraft, the same shape and size that they had seen outside started to land on top of the pyramids. Little legs unfolded from the underside of the flying saucers allowing the spacecraft to cling on to the pointy tops of the pyramids. They were classic flying saucers, round, disk-like shapes and domes on top.

Jess looked up, took one look at the phone and turned back to Frankie again, her sobs turning into full crying.

"I knew the pyramids were made by aliens!" Chloe yelled as she held up her phone for all to see.

Chapter 5

The classroom was quiet as everyone scanned social networks, watching and sharing different videos from around the world.

It was interesting to see how different people reacted. Sophia was worried, she didn't really know what was going on or how to react. Kevin knew what was going on and he was even more worried. Chloe was excited. She didn't believe the aliens were here to harm us and she was busy thinking about the new technologies they would bring with them.

Mrs Smith had left the classroom to attend an emergency teacher meeting in the corridor, but nobody had noticed, everyone was too busy watching the aliens.

The door handle turned, and Sophia let out a scream as she reacted to the squeaking door. Mrs Smith entered, white and pale with a nervous expression on her face.

"Is everything okay Miss?" Marko asked as the class went quiet, waiting for an announcement.

"Yes, thank you Marko." Mrs Smith replied. "Class, we are to remain in this classroom until further notice. We don't know what is happening outside and we don't want to cause anyone any distress."

"We know what's happening." A voice came from the back of the class, holding up a mobile phone. "It's aliens, they are invading."

A few mumbles and small yelps crossed the classroom before all eyes turned back to the teacher.

"I have taught you not to believe everything you read on the internet?" Mrs Smith argued as she turned on the projector. "Let's see what the proper news has to say about this."

A few moments passed while the computer started up and Mrs Smith found the daily news page. There was nothing there about aliens or flying saucers. The front page acted like nothing strange was happening at all.

"No offence Mrs Smith." Chloe started. "But social media news travels much faster, look."

Chloe turned the phone around displaying a selection of live videos from all around the world. Many of the streams showed the strange craft in the air and some of them had started to land.

"Class, I am not going to stop you from watching anything on your phones, but please remember that there are people here who are scared." Mrs Smith announced this as she looked down at Jess. "Please be careful with the information you share with the class."

"Chloe, what have you discovered?" Sophia whispered as they all huddled around Frankie's desk.

"The UFO's are everywhere, over the USA, Russia, China, even in Antarctica." She updated the group without taking her eyes off her phone screen.

"They are starting to land in various places around the world too." Marko added as he tapped the screen on his phone. "In Egypt and Israel at the moment."

"All the world armies have been mobilised." Kevin added, showing tanks rolling through various cities around the world.

"Still think it's the Australians?" Frankie whispered to Chloe.

"I don't know what to think." Chloe whispered, the fear, mixed with excitement, could be heard in her voice as she stared at her screen.

"Everybody, look at this." Marko said as he held his phone to the group.

On the little screen was an image of Big Ben in London. Someone was recording from across the river as a huge, silver spacecraft blocked the bridge that led to the large clock. A tube lowered from the middle of the space craft and three little figures appeared on the road.

They were small compared to the cars around them, they resembled children dressed up on Halloween night and they were clearly chatting to each other, but the camera was too far away to hear anything. They each wore little red space suits which made their bright green skin stand out.

"What are they?" Sophia asked, breaking the silence as everyone watched, trying to understand what they were witnessing.

"I think they are aliens." Kevin replied.

"Like from TV? I thought aliens were fictional like the Lock Ness Monster or dragons." Sophia asked again.

"If they are made up this is the best prank in history, or they are real?" Frankie answered.

"What are they doing?" Jess asked, peeping up from Frankie's chest and pulling her ginger hair away from her face long enough to see what was going on.

"They are just talking." Chloe said as she pointed to the phone, tapping on the aliens to zoom in on them.

At that moment, a nearby car that had been parked on the bridge swung its door open and a middle-aged woman quickly got out and started to run. The little green aliens jumped in alarm at the movement and then started to shout something at the woman who was running away.

"If I didn't know any better, I swear the aliens just asked that woman for directions." Frankie said.

"That's what I heard too." Marko confirmed.

"Aliens that speak English?" Sophia asked.

"I don't know what to believe any more." Chloe added.

Hearing the aliens speaking English, the woman stopped, turned to face them and then froze as they walked up to her, talking over each other and gesturing at places around them.

The camera was too far away to hear clearly what they were saying. Whoever was recording was being careful not to get too close.

The aliens tried to talk to the woman, that was obvious, but the poor lady was frozen to the spot in fear, then, she fainted and collapsed onto the floor.

"They killed her!" Sophia shouted.

"No, they didn't, look again." Marko pointed to the aliens.

The three aliens were now arguing with each other. It looked like they were blaming each other for scaring the woman.

The little green men walked over to her body and started to lift her up. It took all three of them to drag her to the side of the bridge before they started wafting her with their large, webbed hands.

"They are trying to calm her down." Chloe said.

"They need to splash her with water." Kevin added.

Then, as if on cue, one of the aliens sat down on the side of the road next to her, pointing its two antennae towards the woman. Green liquid oozed out of the two stalks on top of its head and splashed straight into the woman's face

"That's disgusting." Sophia said, recoiling at the sight. "I would rather die than be hit with alien juice!"

"It worked, look, she is waking up." Kevin announced.

The woman wiped the liquid off her face, opened her eyes and saw the three little aliens surrounding her. She opened her mouth to scream but before any sound could come out, she fainted, again.

They started to fight and shout at each other, gesturing at the woman who was slumped on the floor. Then one of them noticed the person on the far side of the bridge, recording them. Immediately they all started to run at the camera, causing whoever was holding it to back up and run away.

Just before the live video ended the aliens could just be heard shouting 'Wait, we just want to visit your museum.'

"What have we just witnessed?" Marko asked as he put away the blank screen.

"Was that first contact?" Chloe asked.

"Well, let's try to sum it up. Aliens have landed on Earth; they want to visit museums and they can speak English!" Frankie said in a panicked tone.

"I don't think they just speak English." Chloe said as she put her phone in the middle of the group. It displayed a similar alien spacecraft, three more aliens in the middle of a city, a little caption in the top corner indicated that it was Hong Kong, and these three aliens were trying their hardest to get closer to the crowd that was now running away from them. They were shouting something that sounded like Chinese.

"Of course, they must have some sort of universal translator." Chloe figured as she watched the Chinese speaking aliens chase the crowd through the streets.

"Check out the situation in Paris." Kevin said. Everyone started to tap on their screens to bring up live feeds from various places around the French capital.

Multiple silver discs were hovering over the city. One was orbiting around the Eifel Tower while others were finding parks and grassy areas to land.

"One is landing at the Louvre Museum." Chloe said.

It was sunny in Paris and the Louvre Museum, one of the most visited places on the planet, was covered with people. As soon as the aliens appeared in the sky people started to live stream the event, initially thinking it was some sort of artwork or performance.

It was very easy to find videos from multiple angles showing one of the spacecraft lowering itself. Little legs started to appear underneath, and just like in Egypt the spacecraft tried to land on the large glass pyramid at the front of the museum.

"That glass won't hold the weight of an entire spaceship." Chloe remarked.

"These are aliens, they must know what they are doing." Marko replied.

As soon as he said this, the alien craft made contact with the glass pyramid and shattered it into millions of pieces that fell into the basement below. The spacecraft lurched as the building crumpled underneath it and instead of landing on the pyramid, the UFO fell from the sky and crash-landed on the ground outside the front of the museum.

"Told you." Chloe grinned.

"I am not so sure these Aliens are as advanced as we might think." Kevin commented.

"I think you might be right. Are you looking at the Eifel Tower?" Frankie said as he turned his phone to the group.

It displayed the lawns underneath the Eifel Tower and a large alien spacecraft sitting next to it. A small group of green-skinned aliens, each with two little antennae sticking out of the top of their heads were huddled nearby, staring at landmarks, pointing and looking like tourists trying to find their way around the city.

"I bet the antennae allow them to speak to whoever they want." Chloe guessed.

"Aww, there is a baby alien with them." Sophia commented at the tiny little alien, dressed in a red suit stood next to the group and holding the skinny hand of one of the adults.

The strange spacemen walked towards a group of tourists who had been hiding behind a stall selling churros. As soon as they noticed they quickly ran away, leaving the Christmas market empty.

The brave cameraman who was hiding behind a fake Christmas tree zoomed in on the aliens as they approached the market. The tiny figures started to look at the goods that were on offer, acting just like tourists.

"What are they doing?" Jess asked as she peered into the phone again.

"They are shopping." Sophia yelled as she recognised the behaviour.

"I don't think so, but they are certainly looking for something." Chloe replied.

The aliens could be seen picking up and examining the miniature Eifel Towers, flicking through the various maps of the city and playing with the snow globes. One of the aliens walked backwards into a stall selling hats, tripped up, fell into them and came out wearing several on its head. The other aliens started to laugh, an ear-piercing sound that was fortunately muffled by the phone speaker.

"These aliens are a bit clumsy." Kevin commented.

"Coming from you that's quite a statement." Sophia poked at her friend. He was about to reply but she briefly lifted her Santa hat to reveal the green hair and he backed down, accepting the punishment.

One of the aliens picked up a large teddy bear and handed it to the child alien that had been following along.

"I think that little one is a child, and it's with their parent." Marko said.

"They are on a family holiday in France?" Sophia asked.

"Either that or it's take your alien child to workday." Frankie joked.

The little alien grabbed at the teddy that was twice its size, softly petted its head and then stuffed the entire bear in its mouth before burping up some of the fluffy guts.

"Well that's disturbing!" Marko said, turning away from the phone.

"Guys, check out Washington D.C." Kevin alerted the group and once again everyone typed into the search and scanned the live videos for anything containing the White House.

"They have knocked over that huge tower!" Sophia was the first to load a video of a guy shouting into the camera and moaning that the aliens knocked over the Washington Monument. The large, white tower lay on the grass in pieces.

"They are hovering over the White House!" Marko shouted.

"The government have scrambled their jets!" Kevin said, showing another video of military planes taking off from an airbase.

"They are shooting at them!" This time it was Chloe that put her phone out for the group to watch. "They are shooting at the aliens."

"Yes, but they haven't actually hit them." Marko pointed to his video. Someone was recording the spacecraft as two fighter planes flew past, firing their machine guns, not a single bullet making contact. The sound of the machine guns was obvious, they were shooting at the silver ships, but no dents or sounds of impact could be heard. The ships continued floating in the sky, like nothing had happened.

"I don't understand, they must have forcefields or something." Chloe tried to explain.

The video spun around and showed another set of planes screaming across the sky at the alien spacecraft. Then plumes of smoke appeared, indicating that they had launched their missiles at the aliens.

"Why must the American government always try to solve things with guns and missiles?" Marko asked.

"Better safe than..." Kevin was stopped mid-sentence as the video showed the missiles approach the spacecraft and fly straight through them.

"The missiles didn't even hit it." Sophia exclaimed.

"They really must be advanced." Chloe said as she watched the missiles fly away into the distance.

The person holding the camera suddenly spun it around to show their shocked face. This caught Chloe by surprise and she dropped her phone.

"I suppose anyone can be both clumsy and smart." Frankie said as he reached down and picked up the phone for Chloe.

Mrs Smith had been noticeably quiet during this time, as she too was looking at the live video feeds and trying to figure out what was going on in the world.

Then the familiar sound of an email chirped at the teacher's computer. She opened it, read it and re-read it before getting to her feet. Everyone leaned in, waiting for the announcement.

"Okay class. I have just been told that you need to phone your parents, tell them that you are safe but that they need to come and pick you up as soon as possible." Mrs Smith said as the room immediately erupted into a panic.

"You're not kicking us out, are you?" Jess asked.

"No, we are not, but your parents need to decide what is best for you!" Mrs Smith explained.

"Don't worry, everything will be fine." Frankie said, trying to calm down his little sister as he started to call his mum. "She will know what to do."

Chapter 6

"Thank you for picking us up Mrs Thomson." Marko said from the back of the minivan. Frankie's mum drove a seven-seater so everyone was able to get inside.

"You're quite welcome." She replied. "Just sit tight and we'll all be home safe and sound soon."

"I hope my bike is going to be fine left at school." Chloe said as the car drove out of the parking lot and she watched her silver mountain bike disappear out of view.

"People have got bigger problems right now." Frankie whispered back to her as he pointed up through the sunroof at the silver disks in the sky.

It was a short distance back to Frankie's house by car, since they didn't have to take the long and winding bus route, but it felt like driving through a war zone. Cars were abandoned, people were out on the street like walking zombies, not sure where to go or what to do. Occasionally a shadow would land on the car as an alien space craft flew overhead.

"That's the eighth one to go past now." Kevin said as he stared up through the sunroof next to Sophia and Marko on the back seat.

"What do you think they want?" Frankie asked the car but immediately noticed his mum looking at him through the mirror, then look at his sister on the front seat. Her eyes said 'don't upset your sister'.

"Everyone seems to think they are searching for something." Chloe said. "They land somewhere, start to look around, they use some devices and scan things, then they get back in their spacecraft and fly away somewhere else and do it all over again."

"What could we possibly have that they are looking for?" Marko wondered as he watched a middle-aged man pull into a driveway, get out of the car and run into the house, all while holding a briefcase over his head to stop any alien attacks. "We aren't exactly advanced."

"I don't know, but I bet the government knows what they want." Chloe replied.

"You're such a conspiracy nut!" Frankie shouted back to her. "When you're not trying to find big-foot your pointing your telescope at the moon to see if we really landed there!"

"I don't believe the theories, I just want to know why the governments keep inventing new ones, why are they trying to distract people with crazy ideas, what are they really hiding?" Chloe argued.

"You guys are crazy." Kevin said. "Firstly, the government isn't organised enough to do all of that. Secondly, you saw the missiles, the government are useless against them. We couldn't even touch them."

"Why don't we help them find what they are looking for?" Jess turned around and asked, innocently. "Then maybe they will just go away."

"Perhaps we will honey." Her mum replied. "Just don't worry, we are nearly home and then we'll be safe until it's all over."

"Thanks again Mrs Thomson." Sophia said this time.

"Don't worry. I know your parents are busy, with them both being police officers. They will pick you up when they are ready but the world needs them right now and you are always welcome with us." Frankie's mum said as she carefully negotiated a driver who was more interested in the sky than the road.

"I'm really grateful too." Chloe said. "I am sure that my mum will be out of surgery soon and I can be out of your way."

"Don't worry about it." Mrs Thomson assured her. "Your mum is going to be in high demand tonight as people start to do crazy things, I've told her your safe with us."

Three boys suddenly shot across the front of the car on their bikes, causing Frankie's mum to slam on the breaks.

"That was Jonny and his friends." Frankie said as he watched them disappear down an alley.

"Well, if he continues riding like that he'll be the next visitor to your mums hospital." Mrs Thomson growled as she resumed the journey home.

"Your parents have such important jobs; my dad is just an embarrassment." Kevin said.

"Hey, your dad has the most important job out of everyone!" Mrs Thomson replied.

"What? Shovelling coal into a furnace? Not exactly a surgeon!" Kevin muttered.

"But if your dad doesn't do that, then the power station won't work and nobody can do their jobs." Chloe reminded him.

"That's right." Mrs Thomson confirmed.

"We'll have fun at my house anyway." Frankie said. We can watch Home Alone and show Chloe what she has been missing.

"That's who you are!" Sophia cried out as she realised what Kevin's costume was about. "Now it makes sense."

"Sometimes I am glad we aren't proper twins." Marko commented at his sister's lack of understanding.

"Kevin, are you sure we don't need to go by the high school and get your brother?" Mrs Thomson asked as she looked through the mirror at the kids in the back.

"No, he's alright, he's gone home to his girlfriend's house." He informed her. "It's where he spends most of his time anyway."

"You never told me your brother had a girlfriend." Sophia said, leaning forward over him.

"What's up, you jealous?" Marko joked.

"Well actually, yes, a little bit." Sophia said proudly.

"Sophia! That's my brother your talking about!" Kevin groaned.

"Hey! Last summer Kevin's brother helped out at the coal yard with his dad and really bulked up shifting all that coal every day. He was always hot but now he's *really* hot!" Sophia said, really emphasizing her words to make Kevin squirm.

"Can we change the subject?" Kevin groaned as the car filled with laughter at his expense.

"What's so funny?" Frankie's mum asked.

"Oh nothing, Kevin likes my sister, but she likes his brother instead." Marko summed up the situation as Kevin sunk back into his seat and went red with embarrassment.

"How do you know that the aliens are looking for something?" Frankie asked Chloe, trying to change the subject for his friend.

"It's on all the social networks, there are loads of theories flying around." Chloe explained.

"Well make the most of it. When we get home I am going to ask you to turn your phones off, I don't think it's good for you to listen to all that rubbish on the internet, not right now." Mrs Thomson explained.

"But mum!" Frankie objected.

"No, I'm not listening. I have a duty to keep you safe and I think it's for the best." She replied, ending the conversation with a look in the mirror at Frankie.

"If only we had the new Mario racing game to play when we get home." Frankie hinted. "Then we wouldn't need our phones."

"I am sorry Frankie, that game has already been sent to Santa." His mum replied.

"I know that, but if we could get it back from Santa and I could open it tonight, we could have a great time and forget about all the aliens." Frankie insisted.

"Frankie, you can't ask Santa to bring a present back before Christmas!" Jess cried out.

"Yeah *Frankie.*" Kevin agreed. "Besides, his sleigh couldn't get through all the UFO's"

It was an innocent comment that silenced the room as reality set in and they remembered where they were.

"You will just have to wait and see." Mrs Thomson said, breaking the tension in the car.

"I really like your hair." Jess said as she stared at Sophia in the mirror.

"Thanks, I'll show you how to curl yours if you like." Sophia said as she reached forward to twist Jess's hair through the headrest. "We could have a proper slumber party while these lot play Mario!"

"That sounds awesome! Mum, can Sophia curl my hair?" Jess asked.

"That sounds like a very kind offer, thank you Sophia." Mrs Thomson said as she smiled at Sophia through the rear-view mirror.

"And maybe we could use your hair dye in the bathroom, and I could go blonde!" Jess suggested excitedly and the whole car went silent, waiting to hear her mum's reaction.

"But I love your ginger hair! I wish my hair was your colour!" Sophia expertly shifted the conversation away from the idea.

"Really? Okay then. We'll just curl it." Jess agreed.

Sophia looked up to see a worried-looking Mrs Thomson mouth the words *'thank you'* back at her.

"I bet you wish your hair was any colour other than green!" Marko whispered to his sister, then he received an elbow to the chest as punishment.

A few minutes later everyone was back at the house and rushing inside.

"Quickly turn the TV on." Frankie said. "The aliens have landed in Dubai."

"I don't think so. You can all help me in the kitchen, how does pizza sound to everyone?" Mrs Thomson asked.

"Sounds good to me." Marko agreed as he followed her through the house.

"Sorry about my mum." Frankie whispered to Chloe as they dumped their bags at the bottom of the stairs.

"Why? She is only doing what she thinks is best, and she is probably right." Chloe replied. "After all, at least she is here for you. My mum would rather stay at the hospital than come home to look after me."

"I don't think that's true; I am sure your mum is worried about you, but she can save a lot of lives tonight, you should be proud of her!" He reminded her.

"Yeah, I guess." She agreed.

As the night continued everyone started to relax and forget about the aliens that were out there in the cold. It was just nice to be surrounded by friends on the last day of school.

"Well it looks like your dad is stuck at work. They have shut down all the bridges." Frankie's mum said as she handed out hot chocolate drinks to everyone.

"Is he going to be safe there?" Frankie asked.

"Yes, they are all hiding in the basement, he'll be home as soon as he can. Is everybody happy and comfortable?"

"Yes, thank you for looking after us tonight." Marko replied as he dipped a giant marshmallow into the drink.

"You have to stop thanking me!" Mrs Thomson blushed. "You are welcome to stay, just let me know if you need anything."

"I don't mind staying the night, I just don't have my night-time routine stuff with me." Sophia said as everyone gathered in the lounge with sleeping bags from the garage, spare quilts and blankets.

"I don't think one night is going to make a difference." Marko said as he started to lay out a large double sheet on the floor.

"A little help please." Kevin shouted as he came down the stairs. It sounded like Kevin, but the only part of him that was visible were his feet, sticking out from the bottom of a walking pile of pillows.

"Kevin, is that you?" Frankie asked.

"Yes, and these pillows are getting heavy!" He shouted back.

"How can pillows be heavy?" Sophia asked as she sat down in a chair and draped a blanket over herself. "You need to grow some muscles, like your brother!"

"You tell me if they are heavy." Kevin said as he waddled into the room and dropped the mountain of pillows over her.

"I assume that these are all for me?" Sophia said as she buried herself in the giant pile and smiled back at him. "Thank you."

"Oh no you don't!" Marko said, racing over to the mountain that covered his sister, grabbing one of the soft cushions and hitting his sister over the head with it, pretending it was an accident.

"Hey!" Sophia moaned as she got up holding a pillow in each hand and started towards her brother.

"You can't threaten me!" Marko shouted as he held up a blanket to protect him from the assault. He was safe from his attacking sister, but another attack hit him from behind.

"Sorry, I couldn't resist." Kevin said as he lowered his hand that held a large white pillow.

"Traitor! I'll show you!" Marko said as he turned to face Kevin with the blanket. As he did this, he took his attention away from his sister who launched her own attack. Jumping on his back and knocking him over, into a pile of sleeping bags.

"You are all going to gang up on me then?" Marko asked as he held up a red bed sheet like a matador in front of a bull, asking them to run at him.

"You need to watch your back." Frankie's voice came from behind. Marko spun around just fast enough to see Frankie lifting a sleeping bag over his head and quickly pull it down over Marko, trapping him inside the woolly prison.

Marko went down to the ground in a fit of laughter, trying to find the way out of the bag, only to receive continuing attacks by Kevin, Frankie and Sophia as they kept up the pillow fight.

"No! Don't! Stop it!" Marko yelled as the cushion attack continued, pinning him to the floor.

"You heard him. Don't stop it!" Frankie giggled as he took aim again with the large pillow.

"Do I want to know what is going on?" Chloe asked as she entered the room and stared at the three of them bashing a sleeping bag that contained Marko, only his feet were visible, hanging out of the bottom.

"Okay, you guys will be safe down here tonight, sleep tight." Frankie's mum said as she followed Chloe into the room and dimmed the light. "Maybe Marko won't survive the night, but four out of five isn't bad."

"He started it." Sophia moaned.

"I'm sure he did." Mrs Thomson agreed. "Well don't stay up too late. Say goodnight Jess."

Jess stood in the doorway watching the antics and then stared upstairs to the cold, dark hallway.

"Mum, can I stay down here?" She pleaded.

"I thought you were going to keep me company tonight?" Mrs Thomson reminded her.

"I know, but you will still have Dexter." Jess looked at the small dog that started to wag its tail at the mention of his name.

"Well, it's not really up to me." Mrs Thomson replied, looking around the room to see if the older kids wanted Frankie's little sister.

"Are you sure you don't want to keep mum company." Frankie asked.

"Or you can stay down here with us, we'll keep you safe." Sophia added, sensing the disappointment on Jess's face.

"Thank you!" Jess said as she ran across the room and started to unfold a blanket.

"Come on Dexter. It's just me and you!" Mrs Thomson said to the Yorkshire terrier at her feet. The little dog ran upstairs ahead of her. "I am just up here if you want anything and tomorrow, when all this has finished you can help me take the old decorations to the charity shop."

"Charity shop?" Marko asked as he finally escaped the thick sleeping bag.

"Yeah, my mum has been collecting peoples old Christmas decorations, the garage is full of them." Frankie explained.

"That's pretty cool." Marko said. "And you're giving them away to charity. I bet we have loads you could have."

"She does it every year, we go and decorate the various homeless charities ready for Christmas." Frankie added. "I am sure your mum already gave us some. Last year she gave us a Christmas themed palm tree."

"Oh yeah, now I remember, it was a banana tree, she had me and Sophia wrapping tinsel around it." Marko remembered.

"Let's hope the aliens have found what they are looking for and have left by the morning!"

Chapter 7

The fire had died down and left a low glow over the room that was only matched by the TV, paused mid-race while everyone took a break.

Marko had won the last three races and now he was boasting that he was unstoppable. Frankie's eyes momentarily glanced towards the sleeping bag, wondering if he should trap Marko inside again. The thought soon left his mind as he sipped at his third hot chocolate of the night.

"What did you put on your list to Santa?" Sophia asked as she sat braiding Jess's hair while they waited for their turn in the race.

"I really want a mobile phone. Mum says I am too young but now I'm at middle school I hope Santa thinks I am old enough." Jess replied excitedly.

"Wow, a mobile phone, that's a big responsibility." Sophia said as she reached for a hair bobble. "What do you want a mobile phone for?"

"I want to play games and chat to my friends." Jess replied. "All my friends have one and they are always talking to each other."

"Well you'll have to see what Santa brings you, if you think you're old enough for it." Sophia said.

"Do you think Santa will come if the aliens are still here?" Jess asked.

Sophia looked up as everyone in the room looked at each other, not really sure how to answer that question. In the end all eyes turned to Frankie to be the big brother.

"I am sure everything will be fine. It's still a few days from Christmas, I am sure the aliens will find what they are looking for and leave." Frankie said.

"I agree. I have been watching some videos and they don't seem dangerous. Not like the aliens in the movies." Kevin added as he sent a playlist of clips to the television. "Check this video out."

On the TV a group of aliens were walking down a street, possibly somewhere in Europe near a ski slope. The road went up a steep hill and the ground was frosty. Wooden lodges with large windows filled with ski equipment surrounded the little green men. As the group made their way up to the top of the empty road, they stared into many of the shop windows, admiring the goods on offer.

Occasionally they would stop and stand in front of the trees that lined the street. The would gesture wave at the branches. Frankie was sure they were trying to talk to the mighty oaks.

It was dark and the streetlights glared, making their green skin shimmer. These aliens were wearing blue space suits with chrome details around the collar and cuffs but otherwise they looked the same as all the others.

When they neared the top of the street the camera moved to get a better view. It was obvious it was a CCTV camera from inside a shop and someone was controlling it.

This caught the alien's attention and they headed towards the camera. They started to cross the road to investigate but as they did, two of the five slipped on a patch of ice and slid down the steep hill, all the way to the bottom.

The other aliens watched and started to laugh as their companions climbed to their feet and began their way back up the steep street.

"See, they aren't that advanced, they still slip on ice." Kevin explained.

"Perhaps they come from a planet where they don't get ice." Chloe suggested.

"What are they doing now?" Sophia asked, still watching the aliens on the screen.

The two that had fallen were angry, stomping their feet and clearly throwing a tantrum like children. The other aliens were still laughing, that ear-splitting sound.

Without warning the two angry aliens took something out of their pockets, pointed it at their friends and disintegrated them.

"Woah! Turn it off." Marko said, looking at Jess who was wide eyed at the sight of the aliens disappearing into clouds of green mist.

"Did they just shoot their friends?" Jess asked.

"No, I am sure they just teleported them away somewhere." Frankie said, looking around the room for any better suggestions.

"That's probably it." Chloe agreed. "They must have the ability to teleport."

Kevin fiddled with his phone and pressed the button to load the next video before the scene could get worse.

"This one is better." He said.

The TV switched inputs to show a night-vision camera inside a cinema screen. The seats were packed with people, clearly this was earlier in the day and they had no idea what was going on outside.

Nothing happened for a few moments, then, aliens started to make their way into the dark room. They appeared at the back, in the projector window, casting shadows over the screen.

People started to complain and look back to see what was happening. As they did, fear appeared on their faces when they saw the aliens dangling out of the projector hole on the rear wall.

The cinema soon emptied with people screaming and running for their lives, leaving the aliens alone. They sat down and started to watch the rest of the movie, even eating popcorn that had been left.

It wasn't possible to see what was on the screen but moments later something scared the aliens causing them to jump and throw popcorn all over the place.

One of the aliens took out the same device, pointed it at the screen and a small explosion shook the camera, just before the video cut out.

"What do you think scared them?" Sophia asked.

"I don't know, the only movies that are out are Christmas ones, unless they are scared of reindeer?" Kevin replied.

Dexter, the little dog suddenly woke up and barked loudly, making everyone in the room jump.

"I thought you were upstairs?" Frankie asked as he got up to let the dog out.

Dexter was staring at the front door and as Frankie got closer, the little dog started to growl at something rattling outside.

"Hey boy, it's only the wind." Frankie said as he approached the little, shaking terrier.

Then, just as he was about to pick up Dexter, he noticed the door handle move. Slowly it twisted and clearly someone was on the other side, trying to get in.

"Everybody get down!" Frankie yelled in a loud whisper. "There is someone at the door."

Everybody turned to look at him as he quickly grabbed Dexter and ran back to his makeshift bed near the fire. The room went silent except for the creaking of the door handle. Then a bang, as the lock stopped whoever was there from getting inside.

"Could it be your dad trying to get in?" Chloe asked as she peered out from behind a cushion.

"I don't think so, he would have called to say he was coming home." Frankie replied.

Everybody was frozen, staring at the front door and waiting to see what would happen. They didn't have to wait long. After the attempts to open the door had failed, a buzzing vibrated around the room, then a portal opened up within the door and two little aliens stepped through.

Dexter immediately wriggled out of Frankie's arms and ran towards them barking his little head off. That little dog had no fear.

One of the aliens, the slightly taller one, started to bark and growl back at Dexter. The alien made strange facial expressions and finished with a set of whines. Dexter cocked his head to one side, then the other, then he stopped barking and lay down on a blanket before falling instantly to sleep.

"Stop talking to dogs, it'll make you go crazy!" The other alien said.

"I know, I just couldn't help it, he asked me who I was and why I was here, I had to tell him." The other alien replied.

"Just start looking, the scanner says there is a magical item around here somewhere." The first alien ordered.

The two little spacemen were half the size of an average person and other than their green skin and little antennas, they looked like skinny children. However, their heads were strange, large, more egg shaped, with huge black eyes and no hair.

These eyes started scanning the room until they spotted Frankie, lit up by the fire.

"You there, where is the key?" The taller alien asked calmly. Frankie just sat there, completely paralysed with fear as his eyes locked with the aliens.

"Hello?" The alien asked again, trying to get Frankie's attention. "Is there anyone there?"

"He is broken, like most of the creatures on this planet. No one is able to talk to us." The shorter alien said as he stared at the motionless Frankie. "Come on, it must be here somewhere."

"Just vaporise them and we'll search the place." The taller alien said.

A little whine came from Jess on the other side of the room. Sophia had grabbed her mouth and buried her in a blanket.

"I don't think he is the only one here." The alien said as it slowly walked around the sofa and over to the sobbing blanket where Sophia and Jess were hiding.

"Don't go near them!" Marko suddenly said, rising up from behind a chair confidently.

"Told you there was more than one, and this one talks." The taller alien said as he turned to Marko.

"Where is the key?" The shorter alien asked.

"Which key?" Marko replied, confused at the question.

"Maybe it's the translator, just talk slower." The taller alien suggested.

His friend cleared its green throat and prepared to talk much slower.

"Where... is... the... key?" The alien asked again.

"We don't have a key." Chloe said, drawing their attention away from Marko.

"Look, another one." The alien said, pointing to Chloe. "There is a whole litter of them!"

"We don't have any keys, please leave us alone." Frankie said, finally overcoming his fear and finding the ability to talk.

"We know it is here. Just give it to us and we can be on our way." The alien said. Then he reached into his pocket and pulled out a device. The same little device that had created the explosion at the cinema. It looked like a TV remote, with lots of buttons and an antenna at one end.

"We don't know what you are looking for." Frankie said, putting his hands above his head as he saw the device appear from the alien's little hand.

"Do you know what this is?" The alien was starting to get angrier now as it pointed the device around the room. "This will turn your atoms to pure energy. I don't want to use it on you, but if you don't tell me where the key is, I will have no choice."

Frankie looked around at Marko and Chloe.

"We honestly don't know what you are talking about." Chloe replied, her voice starting to shake in terror.

"Fine then." The alien accepted, then pointed the device at the teddy bear that was sat on the sofa and pressed a button. It disappeared, leaving a scorched outline where it had once sat.

"Maybe you don't know where it is, but perhaps your friends do?" The alien walked over to the blanket that covered Sophia and Jess. With its thin finger, the alien started to pull back the cover to reveal them.

Both girls sat wide eyed as they saw the little green figure staring back at them.

"I'll ask you one last time. Where is the key?" The alien pointed the device directly at Jess and her eyes filled with tears.

"If you don't know, then you are no good to us!" The little alien started to press buttons on the device. It started to whir and hum. "You have five seconds."

Jess looked over at Frankie who was once again frozen. Sophia looked at Marko who was reaching for the hot poker from the fire, perhaps he could use it as a weapon if he could reach it in time.

As he reached out his hand, he grasped the metal rod that lay in front of the smouldering fire. His eyes never leaving his sisters.

"Four…" The alien counted down.

Marko tried to lift the poker up and point it at the little creatures, but he couldn't, it was too heavy. He was sure he had a good grip but he let go and tried again. It was still too heavy to move, like something was stood on it. He snapped his head back to look at the fireplace, perhaps it was caught on something.

Then he saw what was stopping it moving. A large black boot with white wool trim stood on top of the metal rod.

"Three…" The countdown continued.

Marko looked up and saw, attached to the boot were red, fur-lined trousers that made their way up to a red jacket and black belt of an overweight man with a large white beard and a red bobble hat.

"Ho. Ho. Ho!" Shouted the man who stood in front of the fire.

Spinning around the aliens took one look at the new person who had just appeared in the room and started to scramble towards the door without looking back.

The way they moved reminded Frankie of old cartoons.

Their feet slipped from underneath them as their bodies tried to move faster than their legs would allow. For a moment, they were stood still as their little space boots struggled to grip the carpet.

Finally, they both ran out of the room, one of them pressing buttons on the device and pointing it at the large front door.

The first alien collided headfirst with the door, its body slamming into the solid wood and falling to the floor. Moments later a portal opened and the second alien jumped over the crumpled body of the first and through the portal. Thin arms of the alien returned, grabbing his partner and dragging him through the portal before it closed.

"Santa!" Jess shouted! "I knew you would save us!"

Chapter 8

Jess ran across the room and gave the red-suited man a huge hug. The tears in her eyes were replaced with smiles and grins as she met her hero and saviour.

"You must be Jessica." Santa stated as he looked around the room at everybody else. "This must be Frankie, your brother, Sophia and…"

Santa looked down to find Marko still holding the fire poker in his hand, underneath his big boot. "Marko, there you are. Chloe, I loved your costume today, and is that Kevin hiding behind the sofa?"

"Hi." He said as he slowly revealed himself from his hiding place in the corner of the room, unsure what to make of this situation.

"Santa. How did you know we needed you?" Jess asked with all the innocence of a child.

"I got your letter." Santa reached into his pocket and pulled out the letter that Jess had written many weeks ago. "It says that you want a mobile phone and a phone case where you can put your lucky six-leaved clover."

"Yes, and I have been really good this year!" Jess said eagerly.

"Do you know how rare six-leaved clovers are?" Santa asked.

"Erm, not really." She replied as she reached into the pocket of her dressing gown and pulled out her laminated one. "But I have Frankie's, he gave it to me for my birthday!"

"Well let me tell you, they are really rare. So rare that only one has ever known to exist. That six-leaved clover in your hands is one of a kind and it is what the aliens are looking for." Santa explained.

"They want my lucky clover?" she asked. "If it makes them happy and they go away I don't mind giving it to them."

"I am sure you don't." Santa chuckled to himself. "But that's the thing, you can't, if they get hold of it, then they will control all the magic on Earth."

"Oh." Jess said as she stared at the little plant in her hands. "Here."

She held out her hand and offered Santa the credit card-sized clover.

"Oh no, you look after it, the key has chosen you." Santa explained.

"Hold on. If that little thing is so important, why is it not locked away in a museum or a bank vault?" Kevin asked, finally emerging from behind the sofa. "Why is the most important thing in the world owned by a little girl?"

"Hello Kevin." Santa said in a soft, calming tone that made everyone relax. "I am sure you have many questions about what is going on. Jess is the current keeper of the key, it has been looked after by children for generations, before Jess had it, Frankie had it."

"I got it from a kid at camp many years ago." Frankie added.

"You see, the key can take many forms, from a sword to a teddy bear. And it has been guarded by children for five hundred years." Santa continued.

"That seems like a bit of a security problem. Who decided that kids are the best people to look after something so important?" Marko asked.

"A long time ago I decided to give Earths key to children to love and care for, that way the joy and innocence of children can spread throughout the world. The magic reflects whoever owns the key." Santa replied.

"But if the aliens want it, they will keep fighting until they get it." Frankie pointed out. "How do we stop them?"

"The magic of the key flows through me, it's what gives me my magic, and it will give me the power to protect the world." Santa explained as he stood up tall with pride. "As long as Jess has the key, the Earth is safe."

"That's great! You go get those aliens!" Marko shouted up from underneath him, still holding on to the metal rod.

"Unfortunately, it doesn't quite work like that. The aliens aren't an army that can be defeated, they can only be stopped by finding their queen and banishing her back to the planet she came from. She and I share the same power."

"You mean she is the Santa from her planet?" Sophia asked as she tried to make sense of all the new information.

"Yes, in a way. Children own the key to Earth, so I take on a form that makes children happy. The clover gives me the power to create my elves and my workshop. If somebody else owned the key, they could use that power to create an army of aliens to conquer other worlds." Santa explained.

"So, you're an alien?" Frankie asked.

"Not at all!" Santa chuckled again. His laughter was infectious, and everybody started to smile. "Every planet has a life force, something that gives it the power to support life. I am the protector for Earth's life force, the alien queen is the protector from her planet, but she has decided to use her power to conquer other planets."

"Let me get this straight. Every planet has a protector, you are ours, and, as long as Jess has the key, you can destroy the queen who is trying to conquer us?" Chloe asked.

"We need to find the queen!" Marko yelled as he finally realised he could let go of the iron rod in his hand and climb to his feet. Marko was tall, but he still looked like a boy compared to Santa.

"That's the plan." Santa confirmed. "If I can get to her, then I can send her away, and she will take all the aliens with her."

"Well what are we waiting for? Let's get looking for that queen. What does she look like?" Chloe asked.

"I don't know. She can change her form to look like anything." Santa admitted. "I have my elves out there looking for her right now, but they haven't found her yet. All I know is, when you see her, you will know she is the queen."

"Well, luckily for you, we live in a world where every alien is currently being recorded with lots of cameras. We can use the social networks to hunt down anything that sounds like it could be the queen." Frankie said confidently.

"Let's get going then!" Chloe agreed. "We can set our phones to search for unusual activities within the aliens and see if that matches anything that a queen would do."

"Thank you for your kind offer, but you need to stay here and protect your little sister. I can get my army of elves to watch the news and find the aliens." Santa insisted.

"No offence Santa, but we are part of this now, besides, who else has the skills to find the strangest stuff on the internet, we are teenagers, it's what we do!" Marko said.

"I guess you're right." Santa sighed.

"What about me? I don't have a phone... Yet." Jess hinted to the big man by the fire who looked down and then knelt next to her.

"Jess, you need to stay here and think happy thoughts. The happier you are the more strength I have. Actually, I have an idea." Santa dropped his sack on the floor, opened it up and grabbed something from inside.

It was an elf. He lifted the little man up and out of the bag. The resemblance to the aliens was clear, they were the same height, except this little man had bells on his shoes and wore a hat rather than antenna on his head. Santa did this twice more until three elves stood in the living room.

"Jess, this is Bushy Evergreen. He built the toy-making machine at my secret factory at the North Pole." Santa said, pointing to the first elf who stood proudly. "Then we have Shinny Upatree, my oldest and dearest friend who helped me build my home in Lapland and finally Sugarplum Mary, she is in charge of sweet treats."

"Would you like some candy floss?" Sugarplum Mary asked Jess as the little elf took off her hat and pulled a bag of pink fluff from it. "Don't worry, it's sugar-free!"

Jess reached out and took the bag of pink fluff from the little elf and looked back up at Santa as she munched on the treat.

"Jess, I want you to stay here with my three top elves who will look after you. Do you think you can do that?" The big man asked.

Slowly Jess nodded her head and stuffed a handful of pink candy floss in her mouth. Santa smiled back at her and then climbed to his feet, turned and faced the group of teenagers.

"What should we do?" Frankie asked.

"You five are now my lead investigators." Santa said, turning around to face Frankie, Chloe, Marko, Sophia and Kevin. "Let's find that queen!"

Chapter 9

It took fifteen minutes to turn Frankie's living room into a command centre for Santa. Marko and Sophia were checking past reports for strange alien sightings. Frankie and Kevin were trying to keep on top of all the new information that was being reported, while Chloe was trying to rig up a system that highlighted where the aliens were on a map on the television.

"I have to admit, this is all very impressive." Santa said as he paced in front of the fire.

"Most of the aliens seem to be around Europe." Chloe said, pointing to the large collection of dots on the screen.

"That makes sense, unfortunately." Santa said.

"Why is that unfortunate?" Marko asked as he stared at his phone for useful information.

"It's unfortunate because that's where there are large collections of old magical objects. Hundreds of years ago European countries tried to conquer the world to find as many magical objects as they could. All the devices from the past." Santa explained.

"From the past? Who else has had your power?" Kevin asked as he reached into the bowl of sweets provided by the little elf lady.

"Oh, many people over the millenniums. Pharaohs in Egypt who used the power to create armies of workers to build the pyramids. Julius Caesar and his

Roman Army, Merlin and King Arthur." Santa went on.

"That's a lot of history! All those people were protectors of the Earth?" Frankie asked.

"A long time ago many people tried and failed at the job. Some people lasted longer than others but eventually the power always looks for someone else."

"How did you get the job?" Sophia asked.

"I was given the power at the fall of the Roman Empire. You might know that I always enjoyed giving presents away and making children happy, so the magic chose me to protect it." Santa explained. "It allows me to try and make everyone happy at least once a year."

"Hold on." Sophia said. "You said something about Merlin and King Arthur, but they came along a thousand years after the Romans."

Everybody stopped what they were doing and stared at Sophia. She was smart, everybody knew that, she always did well on tests at school, but she always played the role of a helpless blonde. To hear her make such a smart and informed comment was as alien as the creatures outside.

"During that time I was looking for a successor, it was the dark ages and I wasn't as powerful, I was helping the magic find someone who could take over when I retire, so I granted Merlin some basic powers." Santa explained as he took a handful of sweets from the bowl next to Kevin. "But instead of using my power for good, he built an army. Lancelot, Galahad and of course the Sword of Excalibur, and with the Knights of the Round Table they decided to hunt down old magical items like the Holy Grail and Noah's Ark. After that I took the power away from them." Santa explained.

"Wow, so you knew King Arthur?" Kevin asked.

"I knew him, he was a nice man, corrupted by power, like most." Santa said as he stuffed a fist of sweets into his mouth.

"What if the aliens find these items? Can they use the magic?" It was Frankie's turn to ask a question.

"Oh no, I took away all the magic from the items as soon as they were found, they are just boring objects in museums now, but people still like to go and see them." Santa explained.

"Well there are some reports of your elves battling with some aliens at the British Museum in London." Frankie said as he tapped on his phone and sent the images to the TV.

It was quiet and dark outside the museum that appeared on the screen. The large, old building sat in the middle of London; quietly unaware it was about to get invaded. Then the camera started to shake as an alien spacecraft slowly came into view and rested on the steps outside.

Slowly the legs tried to level the large spaceship as it slipped on the icy steps before finally finding its footing. Little men in blue suits came down from the tube in the middle, looked around at the deserted streets and made their way into the building.

The video then cut to cameras inside the museum, the large glass roof was lit up and as the aliens entered they looked up admiring the structure. Throughout all of this they were busy talking to each other, chattering away like they were just like all the other tourists.

Eventually one of them then took out a little device and start to scan the large room. A blue laser appeared and danced around every door and object in sight.

Then it stopped on the far side of the room. It was difficult to see what was there through the darkness.

In the shadows something was moving and the aliens took a step back, unsure what they had found. Moments later it was obvious as little men with long hats and striped shirts appeared.

Santa's elves had been waiting for the aliens to make their entrance and they confidently walked across the big hall in the museum. Five aliens against four elves.

"This should be good!" Santa said, excitedly waiting to see his elves in action against the aliens.

"Now!" The elves shouted, getting the aliens attention and running towards them. They ran fast and they got close, really close. The aliens didn't have time to react. As the elves attacked them from the front, three more elves sneaked up from behind almost at the speed of light and tied the aliens up in tinsel.

They were helpless. The aliens struggled to free themselves but they couldn't escape, they were neatly wrapped with bows on their heads and the more they struggled, the tighter the sparkled tinsel got. The seven elves huddled together, high fiving each other and celebrating the capture of the aliens.

As the elves turned their back on the pile of tinsel, a green alien arm burst out holding one of their devices. A button was pressed, a blue light flashed out, across the hall and into one of the elves, a slightly shorter one, who disappeared in an explosion of glitter.

The elves all turned in shock and ran back to the green spacemen. Before they got there the alien turned the device on the trapped group and they all disappeared in a cloud of green steam, leaving a pile of ribbon and tinsel on the floor.

"Santa, what happened? That elf was shot." Jess asked as she watched the screen.

"Oh, don't worry." Santa said as he reached into his sack and pulled out the same elf that had been on the screen in London moments earlier.

"My elves can't die, they just return back to me." Santa said, patting the little elf on his head. "This is Max, he usually makes all the accessories for games consoles, before that he used to make board games but there is not as much demand for those as there once was."

"Nice to meet you." Max said politely.

"Good work in London, now head back to the village and warn the others about those alien devices, see if they can build some shields to stop them." Santa said as he held open his sack.

"Will do!" Max shouted as he dive bombed into the sack and out of sight.

"I have another video you might want to watch." Marko said. "This was from a little while ago."

The screen showed a flying saucer darting around in the sky over Sydney. The video was clearly being filmed by a helicopter that was hovering high over the city. It watched as a UFO flew underneath the famous bridge, around the large opera house and between the tall buildings. The metal ship glowed in the early morning sun.

As the silver disk made its way back over the bridge one more time a group of elves flying on the back of reindeer appeared and started throwing large rolls of wrapping paper over it.

"They are teepeeing the aliens." Marko said with glee.

"What's teepeeing?" Santa asked.

"It's what kids do to houses at Halloween, they throw toilet rolls over the house and cover it in paper." Kevin explained.

"I see, and you do this at Halloween? I don't like Halloween. It makes my naughty list so much longer." Santa explained. "At the north pole we call this wrapping."

Everyone watched as the elves wrapped the alien spacecraft in glittery paper. With every sheet of paper used, the craft got lower in the sky, slowing down, before neatly landing in a nearby park. This allowed the elves to finish the job, putting a large ribbon around the ship and tying a giant bow around it.

"More aliens taken care of." Kevin said triumphantly.

"Yes, but they will keep coming until we find the queen!" Santa explained once again. "We need to get her and stop her magic."

"Hold on, I think I might have something, I think this might be the queen!" Chloe said excitedly to the room.

Chapter 10

"I have been watching the locations that the aliens have visited." Chloe said as she displayed a map of the world on the television. "At first they went to Paris, like every other city. Then they went back a few hours later, then, finally, one big ship landed outside the Louvre Museum about an hour ago."

"Do you think that's the queen?" Marko asked.

"They haven't returned to any other place twice, it's different to anywhere else and that is the biggest ship I have seen. I think it's our best shot." Chloe explained.

"Good work!" The elf known as Sugarplum Mary said. "Here, have some sweets."

Chloe reached into Sugarplums' hat and retrieved a handful of chocolates.

"Thank you." Chloe said as she began to unwrap one. "Wow, these are delicious!"

The three elves had been busy setting up a fort in the living room with Jess. They had hung ribbon from the edges of door frames, windows and the fireplace and crisscrossed it around the room, over everyone's heads. Then they hung blankets from these overhead cables so that a large, tent-like structure was starting to appear. Occasionally something would be required that they didn't have, like pegs to fix the blankets to the ribbon, but the elves would simply dip into their hats and pull out whatever they needed.

Shinny Upatree had just plugged in the fairy lights and now the living room was starting to look really magical. It was certainly keeping Jess happy.

"I think this is your best shot with the queen." Marko said to Santa as he zoomed in on the map.

"Let's get going then." Santa said in his booming voice.

"Hush! You'll wake my mum!" Jess said from inside the blanket tent.

"Don't worry, your mum is fast asleep. Isn't that right?" Santa looked down at Shinny Upatree who took off his hat, went to the bottom of the stairs, pulled out some glitter and gently blew. The glitter floated upwards, over the upstairs landing and into Mrs Thompson's room.

"She will be asleep all night." Shinny said when he returned.

"Come on then, let's get going!" Santa boomed again.

"Erm, what do you mean?" Frankie asked. "We can't come with you."

"Of course you can! You want to go on an adventure and save the world, right?" Santa asked the group.

"Yeah!" Marko said with enthusiasm.

"Erm, maybe." Kevin replied, lacking the energy that Marko had.

"Don't you think we should stay here and protect Jess?" Frankie finally said.

"Don't worry, Jess is in good hands." Santa said as Jess's head popped out from her new blanket castle with a mouth full of sweets.

"I'm fine here!" She said between mouthfuls.

"Then let's get going." Santa urged.

"How exactly do we get to Paris?" Marko asked.

"We'll take the sleigh." Santa replied. "I thought you would know how to fly one. After all, you are dressed like me."

Marko looked down; he was still wearing his green Santa outfit.

"Sorry, never flown a sleigh before."

"Don't worry, I'll show you how. Is everyone ready? Okay then, here we go!" Santa said as he turned to face the fire. He took a deep breath and his entire body turned into sparkling dust that hung in the air for a moment then blew up the chimney.

"What do we do?" Sophia asked.

"Stand in front of the fire." Shinny Upatree shouted from inside of Jess's castle.

"Sure, Why not!" Marko said nervously. He stepped forward over to the fire, stood in front and moments later he too was turned into glitter and sucked up the chimney.

"This better not mess up my hair." Sophia moaned as she followed her brother.

"Bring it on!" Kevin yelled as he ran towards the fireplace and followed his friends in an explosion of sparkling dust.

"You ready?" Chloe asked Frankie as they stood in front of the fire.

"You go, I'll stay here and look after Jess." Frankie insisted.

"I don't think so, come on let's go!" Chloe took Frankie by the hand and dragged him in front of the fire. He stood staring at the embers as they crackled and glowed.

Moments later his view was replaced with the rear end of a reindeer. He found himself sitting in the front seat of the sleigh next to Santa.

"You have real reindeer!" Sophia exclaimed from behind. She was sat between Marko and Kevin.

"What did you expect?" Santa laughed. "A dog with stick on antlers?"

"Nobody ever warns you about how smelly they are in real life." Chloe said as she reached up and held her nose. She was sat to Frankie's right as Santa sat to his left.

"No, I suppose they don't." Santa chuckled to himself as he grabbed the reins and tugged sharply.

Nothing happened.

"Okay, everyone repeat after me, On Dasher!" Santa yelled in his merry voice.

"On Dasher." The group said quietly.

"You're going to have to do better than that! On Dancer!" Santa said, raising the volume of his voice.

"On Dancer." This time the group were louder with more energy.

"On Prancer and Vixen!" Santa yelled again.

"On Prancer and Vixen!" Now everyone was getting into the rhythm, and the words came to them from the back of their memories.

"On Comet. On Cupid. On Donner and Blitzen." Everyone joined in with Santa and the whole sleigh lifted into the air. "I forgot to tell you, I am scared of heights!" Kevin said as he looked down over the edge of the sleigh.

"Don't worry, you won't fall out." Santa reassured him. "Now, to Paris?"

"To Paris." Chloe confirmed, looking at the map on her phone.

Chapter 11

The night was cold, not that Frankie or the gang noticed. Santa's sleigh had excellent built in heaters and cups of hot chocolate available at the push of a button. It was better than a first-class flight.

It didn't take long to cover the hundreds of miles around the globe to France. In fact, to any onlookers the journey was almost instant as they shot by at near light speed. Soon the famous Eiffel tower was in view and Santa slowed the sleigh down and circled the city.

Guards were stood outside the old museum, along with police, the army and several large tanks that were all pointed at the spaceship that had crashed through the glass pyramid at the front of the building.

Most of the guards were stood outside an orange tent that had quickly appeared about an hour after the first alien spacecraft appeared. All around, tall men held large guns in front of red tape that stopped anyone getting near.

If seeing a flying saucer land in Paris wasn't strange enough for one day's work, the police went into shock as eight reindeer pulling a sleigh suddenly appeared through the clouds and made a perfect landing next to the silver UFO.

"Stop right there." A French-accented voice came from a megaphone held by a short, skinny man.

"Don't worry. We are here now, you can relax!" Santa's voice boomed into the night sky, more powerful than the loudspeaker and it caused the military that surrounded the entrance to slowly raise their guns and back away from the red-suited man.

"Santa, I think we should ask them what is going on and how can we help?" Frankie suggested as he climbed out of the sleigh onto the frosty ground.

"I agree, after all, we don't know what we are walking into, it could be dangerous." Kevin added as he slipped slightly when exiting the flying sledge.

"If you insist." Santa agreed. He put his white-gloved hand up in the air for attention and motioned for the man holding the megaphone to walk over from the tent.

The little man who wore a wrinkled suit looked tired. He had been here all night after working hard all day. Clearly, he wasn't sure if Santa was calling him over or if he simply lacked sleep and was imagining the whole thing.

Soon he was nudged forward by his friend and slowly he made his way, ducking underneath the police tape and approaching in front of the reindeer.

"Don't worry Maurice, they don't bite." Santa laughed as he noticed how nervous the middle-aged man was around the large deer.

"Santa, he's French, he probably won't understand English." Chloe pointed out.

"Don't worry dear, I am talking French, so are you, elf magic is translating everything you say." Santa explained.

"I'm speaking French?" Marko asked, listening hard to every word he spoke but it just sounded like English to him.

"I must have been able to speak French all along, because it sounds normal to me." Sophia said as everyone looked at her. No-one had the energy to correct her and explain what was going on.

"Excuse me." Maurice said in a French accent. "How do you know my name?"

"I know a lot more than just your name, Maurice. I know that when you were younger you received a bike one Christmas, and you looked after it so well, you even gave it to your son this year for his birthday." Santa explained.

Maurice's eyes glazed over as he remembered the memories of riding his bike when he was younger. Then he snapped back and looked at Santa with fondness and delight.

"What can we do for you?" Maurice asked as he pulled out a pen and paper ready to take notes.

Santa looked down at Frankie and urged him to speak to the little French police officer, after all, it was his idea to call him over.

"Erm…" Frankie stuttered. "What is the situation inside the museum?"

Maurice looked at the young boy stood in front of him, with a dressing gown around him and a lightsabre in hand. Then he looked back at Santa who urged him to answer the boys' question.

"It appears that they are interested in the Egypt exhibition. However, I must warn you, all our weapons have so far been useless against them, I urge you not to go in there." Maurice said, his eyes trying to alert Frankie to the danger inside the museum.

"Thank you, Maurice, we'll be fine, after all, we have magic on our side." Santa said as he patted the man on the back and thanked him for the information.

Maurice took the hint and quickly scuttled back to his tent, confused by the entire situation. As he passed the reindeer, Blitzen snorted loudly, causing Maurice to jump, turn around, stare at the antlered deer, and then run away twice as fast.

"I told you they would be looking for old magical items." Santa said, turning back to the group.

"What do they want with Egyptian artefacts?" Chloe asked.

"Rameses. He was one of my predecessors, however, he only wanted to use the power to create an empire. He was eventually overthrown and lost his powers." Santa explained.

"The aliens will be after his magical stuff then." Kevin said, standing up straight and preparing himself for the battle.

"They might be but they will be disappointed. I deactivated everything hundreds of years ago, unless something new has been found recently I think we should be safe." Santa said.

"What's the plan?" Marko asked as he looked into the crater where the alien spacecraft was dangling, surrounded by the metal frame of the crumpled glass pyramid that used to stand in front of the museum."

"It's too dangerous to use this entrance." Frankie said as he pointed to the sharp metal beams and wreckage to the escalators and stairs that led down into the basement.

"I know another way in, via the gift shop." Santa explained as he moved towards another set of stairs a little distance away. "Just be careful, move slowly and tell me if you see any aliens."

The teenagers all looked at each other, then followed the large, bearded man.

The stairwell was tricky, it was open to the outside weather, no doors or roof, which meant the stairs were covered in a thin layer of ice and everyone gripped the frozen handrails to avoid slipping.

The police had cut the power, so it was completely dark. Further ahead the emergency lights lit up the small shopping area that had been built in the basement.

There was no movement, everything was spookily quiet, even the chattering of the police above them drifted away as they went below ground.

Holding onto the railings the gang slowly inched their way down, taking each step slowly, only to be bypassed by Santa who sat on the handrail and slid down into the darkness, letting out a joyous laugh as he went past.

He landed at the bottom with both boots letting out a large thud and cracking the ice. Santa meant business and he wanted any nearby aliens to know he was here.

This gave everyone else confidence. If Santa wanted to act tough, then they could also be brave. The five of them ran down the stairs to catch up with Santa. Marko led the way and Kevin made up the rear. Marko jumped down, copying Santa and landing loudly on the marble floor. Everyone else followed, Frankie, Chloe and Sophia all landed with thuds to signal that they had arrived.

Finally Kevin jumped off the last step preparing to land next to Sophia. His shoes hit the polished floor but he didn't notice the thin layer of ice. As soon as his feet made contact, they slipped out from under him and he landed in a crumpled heap.

Sophia was the first to turn around and upon seeing Kevin lying on the floor she couldn't help but let out a little giggle as she helped him up.

"Go on, everyone have a laugh at my landing." Kevin instructed as he dusted himself off before making his way over to Santa who was stood next to a map of the museum.

"It seems the Egyptian sector is on the far side, up the stairs, past the Romans, through the Ancient Greeks and straight ahead. It'll be like walking back through time." Sophia said, pointing to the map.

"Good work sis, now everyone needs to be careful, aliens could be anywhere, isn't that right Santa?" Marko asked as he took the lead.

"That's right, be careful, and if you see anything let me know!" Santa instructed as he pulled his gloves tight.

The underground mall was dimly lit and the group found it best to walk in a circle, backs together, looking around for anything unusual. This meant that Kevin, at the rear, found himself walking backwards a lot.

"Watch out for the…" Chloe tried to warn him, but it was too late.

In the middle of the shopping area, a small pond was set up where people could throw coins and make wishes. Kevin didn't see it, he walked backwards, straight into the side, fell back and landed with a splash in the shallow water.

He heard everyone laughing around him. He reached out and caught a hand that pulled him out. It was Sophia's.

"Thanks." He said as he stood there, soaked, his red woollen jumper stretching from the weight of the water.

"Don't worry." Santa said as he reached into his jacket pocket and pulled out a handful of sparkling dust.

He held it up to his mouth and blew. The dust floated around Kevin and started to shine bright, incredibly bright, and Kevin felt like he was in a sauna. The light wasn't blinding but it did warm him up and dry him. Moments later the dust settled on the ground and Kevin realised he was no longer wet.

"Thank you!" Kevin said to Santa. "Is there any way we can get more light around here? I can't see where I am going, how am I ever going to spot any aliens?"

"Now that's a good idea." Santa chuckled to himself as he reached back into his coat, pulled out more dust, brought it up to his bearded face and blew.

The dust flew out of his glove and slowly floated around the entire museum, disappearing down distant corridors, glistening as it went. Each speck of dust glowed with an orange warmth as it started to settle on the lights overhead.

Moments later the large gold and glass chandeliers above them lit up and cast everywhere in a soft, yellow light.

"Over there!" Sophia shouted as the surroundings became visible.

"What is it?" Marko asked as he threw up his arms ready for a fight. Instead of aliens, he watched his sister run across the marbled floor and towards a shop window.

On display were a series of makeup and cleansing tools from a beauty store with strange mannequins in the window.

"This stuff is really expensive! It's made from charcoal. It's the best cleanser on the market!" Sophia said excitedly.

"So, you didn't see any aliens?" Chloe asked.

"What, no, this stuff is much better!" She replied.

"Only you can come to one of the world's best museums and get excited about the shops." Marko said, pulling his sister away from the storefront.

"Santa, that's what I want for Christmas!" Sophia said as she turned to the big guy.

"Come on, we have a world to save first." Marko said, as he walked over to the only staircase that wasn't covered in glass underneath the broken pyramid.

Everyone followed with Santa covering the rear of the group. At least they could see now, but it was still too quiet, uncomfortably quiet and it felt like aliens were about to leap out from behind every corner.

As they entered the Roman area, they noticed the tell-tale signs that aliens had been here. Trashcans were pushed over, their contents spilt everywhere, and some of the statues had been turned around so they looked like they were kissing each other.

Slowly everyone walked down a corridor lined with the stone heads of Roman Emperors. Unfortunately, they didn't have time to learn the names, or even look at the faces of the heads.

If they had, they would have noticed that one of them looked like Frankie, or at least how Frankie might look in twenty years' time. Instead they passed through the hallway without any comment and into a room of statues.

"The craftsmanship on these sculptures is amazing." Frankie said as they slowly walked through the impressive room.

"They aren't that good." Santa said, "That is meant to be Emperor Trajan, but it looks nothing like him."

"You knew these people?" Chloe asked.

"Know them, who do you think gave me my powers in the first place!" Santa said, chuckling at the memories.

"Quiet!" Marko said as he held up a hand and signalled everyone to stop. In front of them two little green men walked ahead, they hadn't noticed the large group following them.

They were too busy carrying a heap of clothes that they had found in the giftshops. They turned into a side room and out of sight.

"What do you think they want all those clothes for?" Chloe asked.

"I don't know, perhaps they are having a fashion parade." Sophia suggested.

The group sneaked up on the entrance. They would have to run past it quickly if they didn't want to be noticed.

"Wait for it." Marko whispered as he held up his hand. "Okay, let's go!"

He quietly led the group past the opening to the room. He made it halfway across, then he made the mistake of looking inside and couldn't believe what he saw.

Chapter 12

Inside the little room, there were more statues, lots of statues, and the aliens were busy dressing them up in modern clothing. Roman statues with denim jeans and cotton t-shirts was a sight strange enough to stop Marko in his tracks. Unfortunately, the rest of the group didn't notice and crashed into him. Everyone tripped over Marko and fell to the floor loudly, getting the aliens attention.

"Santa, what should we do?" Frankie asked as the aliens turned and started walking towards them.

"Here, use this." Santa said as he reached into his sack and pulled out a catapult, handing it to Frankie along with two little toy trolls with green and blue hair. "Fire these at them."

"I remember them!" Chloe smiled at the sight of the little figures that she used to collect.

"Me too, those things gave me nightmares." Sophia commented as she looked away from the little demon trolls.

Frankie lined up the shot, slipped the first troll into the little basket and pulled back on the rubber catapult. He held his breath and let go.

The doll was flung into the room of statues. Frankie was sure he had missed, the troll seemed to be heading straight for one of the larger statues to the left. At the last minute it swerved and changed direction. Frankie was sure he could see the little toys arms and legs moving around to help it move in the air.

It turned into a direct hit on the little alien. The troll instantly came alive and started to scramble around the alien's body. The green faced; big eyed alien almost looked shocked at the little creature that was scampering around its body.

Then, with its face full of rage the troll appeared on the alien's head holding wires that it had pulled from the back of the green man's spacesuit. The other alien tried to swipe at the toy creature, but it was too slow.

The little troll put the wires in its mouth and started to chomp. Electricity sparked up and down the troll's body, through its hair and back to the alien that suddenly vanished in a green mist.

The second alien witnessed all of this and started to reach for its device that hung on the side of its space suit.

"Quickly Frankie!" Chloe yelled, pointing at the second alien.

Once again Frankie took aim and fired across the small distance between them. Once again the troll swerved and made a direct hit with the remaining green creature. It landed on the device that the alien had started to point back at Frankie.

The alien was shocked at the little monster that had appeared in front of him. Pointing the device at the troll, it fired laser beams, but again, was too slow.

Statues all around started to explode as blue beams of energy hit them and then, as quickly as it had started, the mayhem stopped.

The troll had somehow managed to get control of the strange, mobile phone shaped device the alien was holding. The little toy was the same size as the device but it still managed to point it at the aliens head and press a button. Another cloud of green mist appeared as the alien disappeared and the device, along with the troll fell to the floor.

"Now, back in the sack." Santa instructed. The two trolls hung their heads, upset that their playtime with the aliens was over and leapt back into the sack. "I really don't like those toys; they creep me out."

"I know!" Sophia agreed.

"They were awesome." Kevin yelled at the strange, alien versus toy fight. "Real fighters!"

"Where did the aliens go?" Frankie asked, looking down at the weapon in his hand. "Did I kill them?"

"No, don't be silly, they have just returned to their queen. Don't forget these aliens are made of magic, they are just like my elves, they cannot be killed." Santa reassured Frankie.

"Here, I think you should take this back." He said, handing back the catapult to Santa.

"Very well, until next time." Santa said as he took it and placed it back into his sack. Then a loud clatter came rattling through the museum and startled everyone.

"Let's keep going." Marko insisted, getting to his feet and following the sounds of aliens up to no good.

Under any other circumstances this would have been a great experience. Inside the Louvre with no-one else around and free to go wherever they like, it would have been a highlight to any vacation. However, with aliens around every corner there was little time to enjoy the exhibits.

"This is the Egyptian section." Marko said as they passed through into the new area. The corridor seemed to change along with the decoration. No longer were they stood in a marble hallway, but instead everything seemed to be made of sandstone, just like being in Egypt.

"I think I can hear something further ahead." Kevin whispered as he started to reach into his satchel. He had never thought of taking it off all night and was still wearing it. He opened one of the pockets and took something out.

"In there." Marko whispered as the group came to a stop outside the archway that led into a side room. There was clattering and banging coming from inside as the group huddled next to the entrance.

"Take a look." Sophia urged her brother.

"You take a look." He argued back.

"I'll take a look." Kevin said as he pushed them both out of the way and stood near the opening. In his hand he revealed what he had removed from his satchel. It was a mirror.

Slowly he held it up in front of the opening so that he could see around the corner and into the room. There were three aliens this time and they were looking at all the items in glass display cases.

One of the aliens was wearing a piece of ancient Egyptian clothing that once hung up on display. It was tatty, had holes all over it and on the tiny creature it looked more like a dress.

Another was looking inside clay pots, emptying the dust from inside onto the floor.

"They need a cleaner around here. Look at all that dust!" Sophia remarked as she watched the scene in the mirror.

"They are jars containing the remains of people, their lungs, liver and stomach." Chloe explained.

"You mean that's dead people's guts? Gross." Sophia replied, turning away from the spectacle.

The final alien was inside a large sarcophagus that stood in the middle of the room. It was difficult to see what it was doing but occasionally little green arms and legs would appear from the stone coffin. After a few moments, the alien jumped out, it had been busy wrapping itself in bandages and now it looked like an alien Egyptian mummy.

The other two aliens, upon seeing this let outbursts of laughter. At least that was what it looked like, but the sound was deafening and terrifying all at the same time. Everyone held their ears to stop the piercing sound, but it was no good.

As the screeching got louder Kevin dropped the mirror. The clatter of it hitting the ground stopped the alien's laughter instantly and they turned to face the door. Everyone held their breath. They had been caught.

"Here, pass this to Kevin." Santa said as he reached into his bag and pulled out a remote-control car. Frankie passed it down the line to Chloe, who, in turn gave it to Sophia, then Marko and finally Kevin.

The car was small but through the windscreen Kevin could see a little camera. On the remote control was a screen, joysticks and a button labelled 'Power' which he pressed, and both the car and controller turned on. Kevin could see his own face staring back at him on the little screen. He was stood looking at the car.

Quickly he put the car on the ground and, watching through the screen, he drove it forward and into the room of Egyptian remains.

The aliens were caught off guard. They did not expect to see a toy racer appear from the main corridor and they started to run away. Kevin was sure he saw a bit of fear in their usually expressionless faces.

"Round them up." Marko said as he watched over Kevin's shoulder.

The car started to approach them, and the aliens began to run and jump over the tables. Keeping up with them, the little car chased them as the aliens fled in panic.

After a couple of laps around the room the aliens finally jumped into the large stone casket in the middle that once contained a real mummy.

"Well done!" Santa said to Kevin as he took a few steps forward and entered the room. Little alien faces peered up from their hiding place to see the giant man dressed in red.

"What do we do now?" Frankie asked as the group followed Santa into the room.

"We put the lid on them." Santa explained as he gestured to the golden sarcophagus lid that stood upright on the far side of the room.

"Santa, that is made of stone and gold, there is no way we can lift it." Marko objected.

"I wasn't expecting you to." Santa replied as he reached into his sack and pulled out two elves.

They wore striped tops, green hats and long shoes with bells on the end. One had a long beard and the other wore a large pink bow on her hat. They didn't need any instructions, as soon as Santa let go of them, they ran over to the stone lid and lifted it like it was made of paper.

"Wow, your elves are super strong!" Sophia said, watching them carry the lid over to the stone case where the aliens were hiding. They lifted it high in the air and dropped it into place, trapping the aliens inside.

"Good work!" Santa praised his little helpers. "This is Jade and her husband Tony."

"Pleased to meet you." The two elves said in unison.

Murmurings from inside the stone box started to get louder as the three aliens started to bang on the walls.

"One moment." Tony said, as he took off his hat, reached inside and pulled out a set of chattering, toy teeth. He turned the key on the side, slid the top off the tomb and dropped the plastic teeth inside before quickly returning the lid.

Everyone stopped and listened as the chattering echoed around, inside the stone box. Then a scrambling as the aliens tried to escape the biting mouth. A few puffs could be heard from inside and then the box went silent again.

"They really have destroyed this room." Chloe noted as she looked around at the destruction of the items on show.

"Do you think this stuff was important?" Frankie wondered.

"Don't tell anyone, but most of this stuff is fake anyway." Santa whispered. "They keep the real stuff in big vaults underground."

"Really, wow." Chloe commented. "Everything is a lie. That's good to know."

"Jade, Tony, take a look around and see if there are any more aliens in the building." Santa instructed his little workers.

"Will do!" They said, high fiving each other and zooming off at what looked like light speed. They covered the entire building in seconds, scanning all remaining rooms for signs of aliens. Moments later they returned.

"The museum is free of aliens." Tony confirmed to Santa.

"If the queen isn't here, then where is she?" Marko asked.

Everyone reached into their pockets, pulled out their phones and started to search for new signs of aliens.

"The largest group of aliens are now in Florida, they are at a theme park." Marko said, holding up his phone for everyone to see.

"That's nothing compared to what is happening in Las Vegas." Frankie argued, putting his phone next to Marko's.

"Which one do we choose?" Kevin asked.

"Well, we are too young to go to Vegas." Sophia added.

"How about we do both." Santa interrupted. "Marko, Sophia and Kevin. You three go with Tony and Jade to Florida, Frankie and Chloe, you can come with me to Las Vegas."

"Sounds like a plan." Marko agreed.

"What happens if we find the queen?" Kevin asked.

"Here, take this." Santa reached into his bag and pulled out a huge radio. It was the type you might see in the army fifty years ago. It was huge, about the size of Sophia's arm and Kevin could barely carry it.

"You can use this to talk to me, it's a walkie talkie. I have the other one so we can talk to each other." Santa explained.

"Erm, no offence Santa but can't we just use our phones to do that?" Marko asked as he compared the size of his little phone to the huge device Santa had given him.

"I suppose you can, maybe I am falling out of touch with the real world these days." Santa considered as he put the giant phone back into his sack.

"Great, we'll call you if we see anything." Marko confirmed. "But how do we get to Florida?"

"That's easy." The little elf known as Jade said. She walked over to an emergency exit door and pushed it open. It revealed the Eiffel tower, neatly lit up in the night sky.

"That's not it." Her husband said, looking into the cold outdoors.

"Hold on a moment." Jade insisted as she shut the door again. She gave a little tap on the handle and opened it again. The sight of a tropical beach met everyone's eyes. The palm trees were swaying and there were people on the sand sunbathing.

"I wouldn't mind relaxing on a beach." Sophia said as she walked towards the door.

"Those aren't people sunbathing, they're aliens, and they are coming this way!" Kevin yelled as Jade once again slammed the door.

"Hold on, I got it this time." She said as she once again tapped on the handle then opened the door.

This time the unmistakable sight of a large white castle, Cinderella's castle, in The Magic Kingdom at Disney World appeared. It was night-time, the park was quiet, except for the UFO's that flew overhead.

"Alright! I've always wanted to go to Disney!" Sophia said as she walked through the door, followed by Kevin and her brother.

"Good luck everybody!" Marko shouted as the two elves followed him through and shut the door.

"We'll take the sleigh. I think we are going to need it." Santa said as he turned to Chloe and Frankie who were still staring at the door in amazement.

Chapter 13

If you have never been to Las Vegas, it is a strange place for a child to visit. The whole place is designed purely to take your money. However, they know that people are not going to drive into the middle of the desert just to empty their wallets, so they try to make it more interesting.

They built huge casinos with all kinds of strange attractions to distract you, so losing all your money does not seem too bad.

There are miniature versions of New York, Paris and Venice. Hotels are themed like a medieval castle, ancient Rome and Pirates of the Caribbean. To keep people entertained there are huge fountains that dance to music, volcanos that erupt every hour, indoor theme parks, aquariums, theatres, boat rides, sports arenas and even a huge Ferris wheel.

There is so much to do around Las Vegas you rarely notice that the casinos are also everywhere, so you always have an opportunity to lose your money. Whether you are waiting to catch a plane, sitting down at a restaurant, or even going to the toilet, there will always be a slot machine ready.

As Frankie and Chloe flew overhead in the sleigh, they noticed that the sun had only just set, a dim glow was still on the horizon. It was hard to keep track of time when you could fly from one continent to another this quickly.

Santa approached the city from the south, watching the city rise out of the desert was quite majestic for Frankie. The first thing he noticed was the large spaceship sitting on top of the huge, black, pyramid-shaped casino.

"They seem to really like pyramids." Frankie noted as they got closer.

"Perhaps on their world, landing spots are pyramid-shaped, in the same way we paint a giant 'H' on the ground where we want helicopters to land." Chloe suggested.

It was a good idea. The aliens thought we built specific landing spots to help them find what they were looking for. Little did Chloe know; she was absolutely correct with this idea.

Santa guided the reindeer down the main street in Las Vegas as they looked for aliens. The streets were deserted as everyone was hiding from the invading spacemen. There were lots of people recording the sleigh from their hotel windows, even during an alien attack it was never boring in Vegas.

"Over there, in the fountains." Chloe shouted as she spotted the unusual activity they were looking for.

On any normal night, in front of the pyramid-shaped, Egyptian themed hotel a replica of the sphynx welcomed guests. A giant, one-hundred-meter-long lion with the head of a pharaoh sat at the entrance. However, tonight it was missing, although it wasn't too far away. Chloe had spotted it playing in the fountains at the Bellagio hotel.

"How is that even possible?" Chloe asked as she stared in disbelief at the giant cat-like creature bouncing in and out of the gushing water.

"Anything is possible." Santa said as he swung the sleigh out of the sky and started to float around the strange concrete creature. "It means that the queen must be around here somewhere, only she would have the power to bring something that big to life."

"How do we stop it?" Chloe asked.

"I have an idea." Frankie suggested, "I think it might work."

The giant cat looked up from the fountain and noticed the reindeer flying around overhead. Slowly it stalked the sleigh, hiding between the large hotel buildings before leaping onto the fake Eifel Tower outside a French-themed casino. It stuck out a paw to try and grab the sledge as it whizzed by.

"Hold on." Santa shouted as he took emergency action to steer away from the attacking animal. Flying up and out of reach.

The cat tried to follow Santa and leapt into the air, the force of the giant cat leaving the tower crumpled below. Thanks to some clever flying by Santa, the cat missed the sleigh and landed heavily on a nearby hotel roof, crashing through the top few floors before getting back to its feet.

"We need to get it away from the city before it kills someone." Chloe yelled.

"Santa, can your sack create tinsel." Frankie asked.

"My sack can create the best tinsel ever made, why what do you have in mind?" Santa asked as Frankie sat there grinning.

Moments later he had everything in place. A huge piece of glittering string hung from the back of the sleigh and Santa lined up for one more fly by.

"My aunty has a cat and it will chase string around all day long. Let's see if this works." Frankie shouted as he crossed his fingers and looked over the side, down onto the city and watched, hoping the creature would start to follow them.

As the reindeer flew overhead the giant Christmas decoration hung below, twinkling in the sunset. Frankie had never seen tinsel this big or this long. It was at least a hundred meters and as he pulled, more came out of Santa's sack. A never-ending piece of string.

Santa flew past the giant cat and hit it in the face with the dangling rope, getting its attention. The cat did what every cat does in this situation, it leapt, and with both paws tried to catch the sparkly string.

Santa was too fast, too good of a pilot, and the cat missed. It looked up, spotted the tinsel again and leapt once more, nearly catching it but again, just missing. It was working, they had the cat's attention.

"Quickly, head over to the airport, that should give us plenty of space." Frankie yelled to Santa.

"Hold on." He pulled on the reins and the whole world twisted around as the reindeer changed direction and headed towards the large open runways of the airport.

"Ready?" Frankie shouted to Chloe as they both reached into the sack and prepared themselves.

"Ready!" She smiled back.

"One!" He yelled.

"Two!" She replied.

"Three!" They both grunted together as they reached inside the bag and dragged out a giant ball of wool. They rolled it overboard and watched as it fell to the ground below. It wasn't that big when it left the sack, but it grew as it fell, until it hit the runway, bounced with a soft landing and rolled to a stop, ten times bigger. Moments later a giant cat pounced on it and started to push it around the airstrip.

Santa circled the airport a few times as they watched the cat playing, throwing the giant ball in the air and chasing after it down the runways. Eventually, the cat started to run out of energy, it slowed, and finally stopped, lay down on the floor next to a huge aeroplane, curled up and fell asleep, using the giant wool ball as a pillow for its head.

"Great work!" Santa shouted. "That's really creative!"

"Thanks!" Frankie said, blushing at the compliment. "Now we just have to find the Queen."

Santa put the sleigh down in the car park of the pyramid-shaped hotel. Above them a giant silver UFO sat on top of the casino,

"This must be the place." Frankie said as they jumped out of the sleigh.

"I thought it would be warmer than this." Chloe said, as she held her arms close and started to shiver.

"Just because we are in the desert doesn't mean it's warm, it's still Christmas time." Frankie reminded her. "Here, take my dressing gown."

Frankie took off his Jedi gown and wrapped it around his friend. Immediately Chloe started to warm up and she smiled back at her knight.

"Won't you be cold though?" She asked.

"Don't worry about me." Frankie replied, already feeling the cold air but trying not to let it affect him. He looked at Santa who had a knowing smile on his face.

Around them the curtains of the windows in the hotels twitched as everyone held up their cameras and recorded Santa parking his sled at a Las Vegas hotel underneath a huge UFO.

"Come on, let's get inside before we make it onto the news." Frankie suggested as they ran towards the nearest door.

Chapter 14

Disney World, the most magical place on Earth. That was how it was advertised on the TV, and tonight, it possibly was.

The sky was dark, filled with twinkling stars and flying saucers. Distant music played from the various rides but there was nobody to hear it. Normally an army of cleaners would appear at the end of the night to remove the rubbish left after the fireworks show.

Tonight was different, the park had been abandoned as people ran away in panic from the alien spacecraft and the little green men. No cleaners had arrived to remove the mess, the rides weren't even turned off.

Sophia counted at least five spaceships had landed inside the park, based on the video of a drone that flew overhead about an hour ago, although that number was likely a lot higher now.

Marko, Kevin, Sophia and the two elves appeared from one of the shop doors near the entrance to the park. In front of them stood a huge Christmas tree that was still lit up and twinkling in the moonlight.

"Here, grab one of these." Kevin said as he walked over to an information booth and grabbed a map of the theme park. It listed all the rides and experiences on offer, and he started to look for anything that might draw the alien's attention.

"What could these aliens be looking for around here?" Marko asked as he opened his own map and started to look for clues.

"I know a couple of details about this place." Sophia said as she looked over Marko's shoulder at the map. "In the Pirates of the Caribbean ride there are real skeletons."

"That's disgusting." Marko stated.

"And there is a hidden room inside the castle that was going to be Walt Disney's personal penthouse." Sophia continued.

"Really? He wanted to live in a theme park?" Kevin asked.

"Apparently. And there is something called Club 33 which is only for famous people, like presidents. There is a secret entrance here." Sophia pointed to a restaurant on the left of the map.

"How do you know all of this?" Kevin asked as he struggled to keep up with everything Sophia was explaining.

"I used to want to be a Disney princess. I was obsessed." She said with a slight embarrassment in her face.

"Used too? Are you sure you still don't want to be a princess?" Marko joked.

"Well who doesn't? I just need to find my prince." She laughed as she looked at the castle that was at the end of the street.

"A prince. Tough luck Kevin." Marko laughed as he prodded his friend who turned red at the idea.

"I think we need to focus." Kevin said as he looked back into his map.

"A secret club only famous people have access too, real bones on a children's ride and a private penthouse inside the castle. I think we should check out the secret clubhouse, it seems like the best shot at finding old, magical items and it's also nearest." Marko suggested. Everyone nodded in agreement.

"Before we set off, Jade and I think it's a good idea to give you something to protect yourselves." Tony said as he pulled off his hat and reached inside.

"Just don't tell Santa." His wife added.

Tony pulled out a plastic toy gun that fired foam darts and handed it to Marko.

"Cool, this is the new Nerf gun, but what good will plastic bullets be against these aliens? We have seen real missiles hit them and not leave a scratch." Marko pointed out as he took the orange plastic gun from the little elf.

"These bullets are magical and will turn aliens into green smoke!" Jade explained excitedly as she handed him a handful of plastic darts.

"Kevin, I want you to take this. Whatever you hit with it will turn magical and defeat any aliens." Tony said as he handed Kevin a baseball bat. It was painted white with pictures of berries, mistletoe and Christmas lights.

"Thanks, but I am not the best at sports, perhaps I should take the gun and Marko should have this?" Kevin suggested as he looked at the bat in his hands and held it awkwardly out in front of him.

"You'll be fine dear." Jade said turning to him. "Give it a go. Hit this apple at that star on the top of that tree."

Jade took a red apple that sat in a nearby stall and pointed to the star on the top of the giant Christmas tree. She threw it at Kevin without warning and he didn't have time to react. He swung the bat and somehow hit the apple. The little red ball flew up into the night sky and smashed into the star just as Jade had suggested.

"Cool. I have never been this good at anything!" Kevin said as he admired the bat in his hand.

"You just have to believe in yourself." Jade explained.

"And for Sophia." Tony reached into his hat again and pulled out a small sack that was overflowing with small, round beads.

"That's great but I don't think I have time to put all these in my hair." Sophia said, unsure what to do with the sack of hundreds of beads in her hand.

"Throw these at the aliens and it will make them disappear." Tony added. "And don't worry, you won't run out, the bag will always make more."

"Thank you." Marko said, holding his gun out ready to fire at something. "Now let's get moving, we need to find the queen."

After a few minutes of walking through the park they found a large, misty lake. The area was deadly silent, and the moon reflected on the mist making it impossible to see very far.

"Quiet, can you hear that?" Sophia whispered.

"It sounds like a steam engine." Kevin replied.

"What around here uses a steam engine?" Marko asked.

The noise grew louder and it seemed to be coming from the misty lake. Everyone walked forward towards the edge listening hard as the sound continued to grow.

"I don't like the sound of this." Jade said, pulling on Tony's arm to hint that they should be getting away and hiding.

"I agree. This doesn't feel good." Kevin said, stepping back with the little elves.

"Wait, I think I can see something." Marko said as he squinted into the mist.

"I see something too." Sophia agreed as they both leaned against the fence trying hard to see through the fog. Then it became clear.

As the clouds parted a large steamboat chugged into view. It was one of the rides from the park, an old boat that floated around the lake showing off the various jungle-themed attractions.

"It must be automatic." Marko said as he turned to face the others. He looked at them as they watched the boat over his shoulder. "Come on, let's get going, I think we made a wrong turn somewhere."

Marko motioned for everyone to move but instead they were rooted to the spot, staring behind him, fear increasing over their faces.

Slowly he turned around to see what was so terrifying. The ship, large and white, had come to a stop near the pier and dozens of aliens were getting off.

"There must be fifty of them!" Sophia gasped.

"Quickly hide! They are coming this way!" Kevin ordered.

"Where?" Sophia and Marko asked at the same time.

"Over here." Tony said loudly as he opened the door to a gift shop behind them.

"Not so loud!" Jade said, as she cupped her husband's mouth.

"Too late, I think you got their attention." Marko shouted as he started to run towards the old cowboy style building. Sophia was following him as the aliens started to point and shout at them.

As soon as everyone was inside Tony slammed the door shut just in time. Several green men crashed into the oak door behind them, slamming their bodies against the wood.

"Now what?" Marko asked.

"We can't stay in here, there has to be a back door." Sophia suggested.

"Yes, but the aliens might be waiting for us." Jade reminded them.

"There is only one option, we fight!" Kevin replied as he held his bat up high. He walked over to a large pile of Disney themed baseballs that sat near the store counter and readied himself.

"Are you sure about this?" Marko asked as he raised his gun to the door and looked at his friend.

"No, but I don't see any other way out." Kevin replied with more determination than Marko had ever seen. Perhaps he had taken Sophia's 'knight' comment seriously.

Marko put a bullet into the toy gun and pulled back on the handle. The two of them stood back-to-back ready to take on the aliens.

"Tony, open the door!" Marko shouted.

Tony did as instructed. He pulled back on the door and a little green hand appeared, slithering through the gap. Marko took aim and shot a dart, a direct hit in the middle finger, causing the entire arm to disintegrate and disappear. A smile appeared on his face. This might be fun after all.

Moments later a green head with large black eyes appeared. It investigated the store, glancing around at the clothing and teddy bears until it saw the three teenagers and two elves.

It was startled to see a baseball flying at its head. A direct hit between its eyes and it too disappeared in a puff of green smoke.

Marko and Kevin looked pleased at each other and then the double doors swung open to reveal dozens of aliens staring back at them.

Marko fired bullets, Kevin hit baseballs and puffs of green smoke appeared in the crowd. But it was not working. There was too many. Marko and Kevin realised they had miscalculated the odds of this battle.

The aliens would easily turn to smoke, but for as many as they hit, two more would replace them from behind.

The aliens quickly entered the store, overwhelming the two boys. This was when Kevin got desperate. He swung the bat into the tower of balls, causing them to explode towards the entrance. Unfortunately, it was a wild shot and all the magic in the world could not get them all on target.

Some of the balls hit the aliens, but most went smashing into the walls, ceiling and through the windows. It was not his best decision, there were lots of aliens left and now he was stuck with nothing else to fire at them.

Marko was also running out of bullets. He had to reload which took precious seconds each time. The aliens were approaching fast and as the panic started to take over he fumbled with the gun and dropped his supply of foam darts across the floor.

Both Kevin and Marko were helpless, staring at the army of aliens that were quickly taking over. They were getting closer, really close, then, finally, Sophia put her hand in her bag of beads and pulled out a handful.

The aliens were now close enough to her that she couldn't miss. With her hand grasping a hundred beads she threw them at the door. The moment each bead hit an alien a burst of green light burned through the little green man, and the alien was no more.

A few more handfuls of beads later and more than half of the aliens were gone.

The rest of the green men stopped, looked at each other and back at the girl who had enough firepower to take them all down. Then they turned and started to run away.

"Nice work sis!" Marko congratulated her as he scooped up his bullets.

"Yeah, I am impressed." Kevin agreed.

"Well you will get yourselves into these situations, it's a good job I was here to save you!" Sophia laughed as she put away the beads and watched the aliens disappear around the corner and out of view. "Who needs a knight anyway?"

"Now where do we go?" Tony asked as he jumped up from behind the counter where he and Jade had been hiding through the battle.

"I think we made a wrong turn somewhere, we should have passed the clubhouse by now." Marko said.

"How can we get lost? Little kids can figure this place out." Kevin pointed out.

"Well they aren't here at night, with aliens trying to kill them!" Marko reminded him as he pulled out the map again. I think we should head to the pirate's ride, it's not far from here. They all agreed and headed out of the little gift shop, leaving the destruction behind.

"Just a moment." Sophia shouted.

"Sophia! Now is not the time to go shopping!" Marko shouted at his sister who was busy trying on sunglasses with cartoon characters etched into their frames.

"Fine. I just thought they made me look cute and they might distract from my green hair!" Sophia moaned, returning the glasses to the stand.

Slowly they walked around the park once again. Knowing that the aliens could be around any corner. Then they heard an unmistakable sound, a sound loved and hated around the world, the theme tune to 'It's A Small World'.

The music wasn't coming from a speaker but instead, was being sung by aliens, in a high-pitched screech. As they sung, they turned the corner, saw the group and dropped their chocolate bars.

"Attack!" Marko shouted, firing his gun at the aliens.

Panic came over the little green men and they ran behind an ice-cream cart for cover. Marko's bullets flew through the air but only managed to hit the cart.

"Kevin, you go left, I'll go right." Marko instructed as they started to approach the trapped aliens. Then the little dessert stand started to move as the aliens pushed it down the road, still using it as a shield.

"Quickly!" Marko ordered as the two boys chased after them.

As they did silver balls started to appear. The aliens were throwing them at Sophia who had to dodge and weave. Twenty of the little balls appeared in only a few seconds and Sophia's dance lessons were all that saved her as she moved out of the way.

"Don't let them balls touch you!" Jade shouted.

Kevin looked back at saw Sophia trying to avoid the balls falling from the sky. Instinctively he ran to her aid. She stepped left, jumped right and then looked up to see one of the small, baseball sized silver balls heading straight for her.

She couldn't move out of the way in time, she was going to get hit. She watched as the ball shined in the moonlight, every moment getting closer. Then, a new object appeared. A white bat smashed the ball away and Kevin stepped in front of her, smashing the balls away with his magical bat.

"Thank you!" Sophia gasped as she looked around for cover.

"Any time!" Kevin smiled back at her in between hits.

"Quickly, underneath here." While Kevin had saved Sophia's life, Marko had grabbed an umbrella from a nearby picnic table. He put it up and used it as a shield from the falling balls.

"We need to get the aliens!" Marko growled.

"Which aliens?" Sophia asked as she looked around.

"They have disappeared!" Tony said as he and Jade joined the three teenagers under the cover of the large umbrella.

Throwing the balls at Sophia had distracted everyone long enough for the aliens run away. The ice cream cart was now on its side with boxes of ice lollies spilling out but there was no sign of the aliens.

"Over there." Sophia shouted as she pointed to the large, cobwebbed mansion to their left. Everyone watched as the aliens disappeared inside.

"Great! A haunted house." Kevin moaned.

"But why go in there?" Sophia asked. "They will be trapped."

"I don't know, but if that is where they are going, then so are we." Marko said, dropping the umbrella and walking confidently over to the spooky building.

Chapter 15

Frankie ran towards the door of the large glass pyramid and was slightly shocked when it opened automatically. He was scared and nervous, so normal things caught him by surprise. He smiled at how silly he was being.

Inside they passed multiple signs stating that you must be over eighteen to enter the casino floor. There was nobody around to stop them. Everybody was hiding in their rooms except for a couple of hardcore gamblers who figured the end of the world was coming, so why not gamble away all their money.

Inside the pyramid was a miniature Egyptian city, with fake buildings, temples and statues all devoted to the various gods of the ancient world.

Frankie and Chloe made it into the centre of the pyramid first, with Santa catching them up. The large man was not built for running, he had eaten too many candy canes.

"If you were an alien queen looking for ancient artefacts in Las Vegas where would you go?" Chloe asked.

"How about in the only place around here that contains real artefacts?" Frankie answered as he pointed at the 'Titanic' exhibition.

"Brilliant!" Chloe said.

Around them, in one of the fake Egyptian building's alarms started to sound. The words 'Jackpot Winner' lit up on screens and fake cheering came out of the speakers.

"Who is still gambling at a time like this?" Frankie asked.

"You'd be surprised." Santa replied, slightly out of breath from the run.

Out of the building that called itself the 'High Rollers' area, stumbled out two little green men holding their entire weight in little plastic counters. They looked pleased with themselves until they saw Santa.

They dropped their winnings, scattering them all over the floor and fled into the Titanic building.

"I keep thinking I am going to wake up at some point." Chloe joked.

"I know what you mean!" Frankie agreed as he watched a coin roll across the floor and hit the side of his foot. "None of this makes sense!"

"Come on, let's go get that queen!" Santa said as he urged them into the museum shaped like a ship.

Inside, display cases contained all kinds of items from the wreckage of the Titanic, everything from playing cards to wine glasses.

"Look, this one has been smashed open." Chloe said as they walked through the exhibit.

"There is something missing, there is meant to be a necklace in here." Frankie pointed to the empty slot where a little plaque described the necklace that was missing. They both turned to Santa, worried expressions on their faces.

"Don't worry. I took away the magic years ago! Now it's just a lump of gold." Santa confirmed.

"What did the magic do?" Frankie asked.

"Whoever wore it could see five minutes into the future."

"A necklace that allows you to see into the future? It's no surprise something like that made it to Las Vegas." Frankie said.

"I bet the casino owner funded the entire exhibit just so they could get hold of it." Chloe suggested.

"Just imagine if you could know the results of any race, card game or slot machine. You could make a fortune." Frankie added.

"You could. But what if you happened to see your own death, in five minutes time?" Santa said.

"Good point. That would be pretty scary." Chloe said as she looked at the empty hole where the necklace once sat. "In fact, it would stop me using it, because you never know what you are going to see."

"Wow, and there was me thinking that there could be no downsides to seeing five minutes into the future, but your right, if someone told me I could, but I might see my own death, I wouldn't." Frankie added.

"Yes, that necklace has been the cause of many futures that were avoidable." Santa said as he urged everyone forward.

"Is the future avoidable?" Chloe asked.

"Well, no, not really. So many people have used that necklace and had a heart attack from the panic of seeing themselves die of a heart attack, or they see their best friend killing them, so they decide to attack first, to try and stop it, which results in their best friend killing them." Santa explained.

"So, the necklace causes the wearers death?" Frankie asked.

"It's impossible to tell, but nobody has seen their future and not had it come true, whether the necklace created the future or just showed what would happen, it's impossible to tell."

As they made their way around the artifacts they came across the famous grand staircase from the main part of the ship.

"It's all broken." Frankie pointed out. The expensive-looking steps were destroyed. The bannister in pieces and the marble flooring cracked, it looked like it had just been lifted out of the wreckage yesterday.

"This sign says it is only a replica." Chloe said. "I bet the queen was here and by the looks of it, she got annoyed when she realised it wasn't the real thing and she destroyed the place."

"The real staircase was made from wood recovered from Sherwood Forest, enchanted to allow Robin Hood and his gang to hide when stealing from the rich." Santa explained. "Although I took away the magic before it was turned into a staircase."

As Santa stood looking at the destroyed replica, two aliens turned the corner and stopped as they saw the back of Frankie's head.

Unfortunately, Frankie wasn't paying them any attention, they were behind him, he wasn't even aware that they were slowly sneaking up on him.

"Where do you think the Queen went?" Chloe asked as she turned to look at her friend.

Before he could reply he saw the brave girl in front of him go wide-eyed in fear. She was staring behind him and that could only mean one thing.

"Look out!" She pushed him away as the aliens fired a laser beam. He crashed to the floor, landing hard and wondering why she had just tackled him, then it became clear.

As he looked back, he saw that Chloe was now in the line of fire and one of the laser beams hit her.

Everything happened in slow motion. The aliens fired the weapon, Chloe turned away and a green light shimmered across her body. One moment she was there, the next, she was gone.

"Chloe!" Frankie shouted as he dived to where she had once been. It was no good, all he did was get the attention of the aliens once more. They turned to him and prepared their weapon. Frankie saw the end of the device light up green and he closed his eyes expecting the worst.

Nothing. That's what he heard. There was nothing, he didn't feel anything and nothing changed. He opened his eyes again to see Santa holding out his hand to help him back to his feet.

"What happened?" Frankie asked, looking around for the aliens.

"Those aliens won't harm you now." Santa said as he held out a snow globe that contained two miniature aliens, trapped inside the glass dome.

The little green men were banging on the glass, demanding to be let out. Santa put them down on the bannister of the broken staircase and turned back to Frankie.

"They killed Chloe!" Frankie screamed, his eyes started to flood as the emotions suddenly hit him hard. One moment his friend was there, the next she was gone, she had saved him, but he would have happily traded places with her.

"Relax. Chloe isn't gone, but we do need to save her." Santa said calmly. "Aliens cannot kill anything, all they have done is send Chloe back to their queen for questioning."

"Why does the queen want Chloe?" Frankie argued, trying to figure out what had happened.

"I think they were after you. You know where the key is, but Chloe saved you." Santa explained.

"We have to save her!" Frankie yelled.

"I know, she should be close, the queen has got to be around here somewhere." The big man said, trying to calm Frankie down.

Frankie noticed the aliens firing laser beams around the glass snow globe, trying to get out. He picked it up and gave it a shake.

The aliens became dizzy and fell over each other as the snow settled around them. Then a rumbling started to shake the entire building, dust fell from the ceiling on to Santa and caused him to sneeze, startling Frankie. He dropped the snow globe and watched it roll away, out of sight.

"The spaceship on the roof! It's taking off! Chloe!" Frankie yelled as he started to run out of the building.

The whole pyramid was shaking as the alien spaceship withdrew its legs and started to hover in the Las Vegas sky.

The casino was large and designed like a maze to keep people inside, but Frankie covered the distance in record time. He ran out of the main doors and into the car park where he could see the saucer-shaped ship lift into the night sky. Santa caught up with him, wheezing and gasping for air.

"I really need to cut down on the snacks." Santa said as he watched the spaceship float away over the hotels. With one hand raised he signalled the sleigh. The reindeer ran across the car park and came to a stop behind him.

"Come on. If we are going to save Chloe we need to get a move on." Santa said, still panting, but Frankie was already jumping into the front seat.

As they rose into the air the alien craft started to accelerate hard. Frankie looked back down on the city and he could just make out the giant sphinx, it was awake again and playing with the ball of yarn, chasing it down the airport runway.

The further away they flew, the slower the cat became. Then, the cat froze up completely, mid leap, right in the middle of the airport. It was made of concrete once again.

Someone was going to have trouble moving that in the morning, Frankie thought. Then his attention turned back to chasing down the queen's ship and saving Chloe.

Chapter 16

"I don't feel great about this." Kevin murmured as they approached the building that was covered in cobwebs and had tombstones in the front garden. It was designed to be scary but now it had real aliens as well.

"If that is where the queen is, then we need to go in." Marko said as he ducked underneath a low hanging, fake spider.

"I know, I understand why we need to go in there, but I am still not happy about it." Kevin explained.

"At least there is no queue." Sophia laughed as they walked through the maze of walkways leading into the house.

"Do you think they will be hiding inside the ride?" Tony asked.

"Only one way to find out." Marko said as they approached the platform to get on.

"Are we actually going to get on this thing?" Kevin asked as he held his bat up, ready for any surprises.

"You bet!" Marko said.

In front of them was a train of two-seater pods that followed a track through the building. Spooky paintings hung on the walls and unlike in the daytime, there was no music playing. The only sounds were of motors, creaking metal and a distant screaming coming from something inside the house.

"I am not going on my own!" Sophia said as they tried to quickly figure out how to fit three people and two elves into a pod designed for two.

"If it's ok with you, Tony and I will stand guard out here." Jade said. "This place gives me the creeps."

"I understand!" Kevin agreed. "I might stay with you!"

"You're coming with us." Marko said, pulling on his friend. "Afterall, how else are you going to protect my sister?"

"Fine!" Kevin agreed as he was pulled towards the ride and was reminded that Sophia was watching. "I think we can all fit inside one of these pods." He said as he jumped inside.

Sophia followed him, sitting in the middle and with a squeeze, Marko added himself to the seat too. The barrier in front of them lowered over their lap and Marko loaded a bullet into his gun.

"You ready for this?" Marko asked.

"Nope!" Kevin replied with his eyes closed.

"Glad to know my knight is here to protect me." Sophia said.

Kevin's eyes opened and looked at the blonde girl sitting next to him. She was talking to a suit of armour hung above them.

"Don't worry, she didn't mean you." Marko joked and Kevin shut his eyes again.

The pod moved away from the platform and into the cobwebbed covered darkness.

"This place gives me the creeps." Kevin said.

"That's the point." Marko reminded him as he raised his gun at a skeleton hanging from the ceiling.

"It wouldn't be too bad, but I know there are aliens in here ready to jump out on us." Sophia whispered.

"Over there." Marko shot into the darkness but his bullet only collided with another suit of armour. The metal clanging as the bullet bounced off.

"I really don't like this." Kevin moaned as the ride once again went quiet.

"There!" It was Sophia this time to throw beads at a ghostly figure, but once again, nothing happened. It was a piece of glass and the beads just bounced off. Everyone started to laugh at how crazy they were behaving. Then, out of the darkness a figure flew at them.

"Attack!" Marko shouted as he fired a bullet at the attacking creature. Sophia threw a handful of beads and Kevin swung the bat above his head, hitting the flying ghost and knocking the mask off the robot.

"This is ridiculous, how can we spot aliens in here." Kevin muttered.

As the car made its way through the ride it came to a fake graveyard. There were headstones and statues everywhere and the lighting made shadows dance around the room.

"Guys, the casket." Kevin whispered.

In front of the cart was an old stone coffin and the fake plastic lid was slowly moving. Kevin started to get up so he could swing his bat.

"I've got you!" Kevin shouted as a thin hand appeared from within the stone box.

He swung his bat and shattered the mechanical hand into hundreds of pieces. Sparks flew out and that part of the graveyard went dark.

"Nice going." Sophia said as Kevin returned to his seat. "We are causing more destruction than the aliens."

They moved around the ride in darkness and then the lighting suddenly flickered back on revealing three faces in front of them.

"I've got you!" Marko shouted as he fired a shot at one of the heads.

"Hey!" Kevin moaned as he looked at his friend through the mirror in front of them. They were travelling sideways and staring at themselves. Ghosts and ghouls were waving them goodbye with big grins on their faces. It was the end of the ride and they hadn't found any aliens.

"I was sure we had trapped them in here." Marko said.

"Look at my hair!" Sophia gasped as she started to adjust her green-blonde curls in the dim light. Both Marko and Kevin turned to look at her and then each other. Kevin smiled and Marko rolled his eyes.

As they all returned their gaze to the mirror in front of them, they saw the little green man, sneaking up from on top of the pod they were sitting in.

At first, they froze. Then Kevin jumped up and hit the alien with the bat. The alien didn't move, but instead turned into a slime and poured down onto Sophia.

"Eww!" Sophia moaned as the slime hit her. "I hate haunted houses!"

"That wasn't part of the ride." Kevin said as he looked down at his friend who was now covered in green slime.

"You mean that was an alien! I am not sure I can cope with this!" Sophia yelled as she pulled large globs of dead alien from her head.

"Kevin don't move!" Marko raised his gun towards his friend and prepared to fire.

"Woah! Calm down. I'm sorry for soaking your sister in alien guts." He pleaded.

The bullet fired, straight passed Kevin's ear and into an alien that was hanging over the exit. The alien turned into more green slime that just happened to cover Sophia even more.

"Nice shot!" Kevin said, impressed.

As the light returned, so did the platform to leave the ride. Sophia was first up out of her seat. Covered in slime.

"I need to get out of here!" Sophia screamed, getting the attention of the two elves that stood at the far end of the room on patrol.

"That's why I don't like haunted houses." Jade said at the sight of Sophia, dripping with slime.

"You're back. I am guessing you got them?" Tony asked as he held back from laughing at Sophia.

"We got them." Marko confirmed. "But no queen."

"Come here, let's clean you up." Jade said to Sophia as the little elf pulled tissues out of her hat. The moment the tissues touched the slime they stuck, like the slime was glue. Jade looked at the boys nervously, she couldn't get the tissues off Sophia's head.

"There we go. As good as new!" Jade lied.

"Does that look better?" Sophia asked as she turned to face the two boys, her head covered in slime and tissue paper.

It took complete self-control for the boys not to burst out laughing when they saw her.

"You look great!" Marko snorted.

"Yeah, beautiful!" Kevin said, holding back a giggle.

"Thank you." Sophia turned back to the elf but as she did, she caught sight of herself in a mirror. "Oh! Will this night ever end!"

"Don't worry, we'll get you cleaned up at some point. Let's get out of here first." Tony suggested as he held open the emergency door. They all left the ride, but not before they had a good laugh at the photograph taken just after Sophia had been covered in slime.

"This is not funny!" She stormed off, stamping her feet. Then she accidentally slipped in her own slime.

"Come on." Kevin held out his hand to help his friend to her feet. She jumped up and gave him a big, slimy hug.

"Thanks, you're such a good friend!" She laughed as she covered Kevin in slime too.

As they left, they could see aliens were riding a rollercoaster in the distance. They had their hands up and were screaming, just like people do.

"I am beginning to think that the queen isn't here. That these aliens are just trying to have a good time." Marko suggested as they made their way along the main path again.

"I am starting to believe you." Kevin agreed.

As they carefully made their way around the park, hiding in the shadows, they watched as the aliens enjoyed the rides. They were on the carousel, the roller coasters and even the teacups.

"We better check out up there." Marko said as he pointed to the large castle on the lake.

"Walt Disney's secret room?" Kevin asked.

"I don't know how we get in there though." Sophia said as she pulled out a map.

"We'll show you!" Jade said as she took them by the hand. "It's been a long time since we were last in there, I wonder what they have done with the place?"

Chapter 17

Santa was a great pilot, as the UFO weaved in and out of the clouds, the sleigh kept chase with ease. Santa barely had to try, almost as if the aliens wanted him to follow them.

The silver ship dove straight into the Grand Canyon and tried to lose Santa between the rocks. Ducking and diving, it was thrilling for Frankie, like being on a rollercoaster, but all he could think about was Chloe.

He was determined. He was going to get his friend back no matter what it took. If the queen was also on that ship then she would pay too, somehow Frankie would make sure of it.

"We could bring them down?" Santa suggested. "Tie them up with tinsel?"

"No. We need to know where the queen is. If she isn't on that ship then they will lead us to her, and to Chloe." Frankie explained.

Bringing the ship down might also put Chloe's life at risk, if she was inside, and he was not prepared to risk that.

As Frankie sat there, watching the world go by, he couldn't help feeling that they were being fooled. That they were being led into a trap. This chase seemed far too easy.

After a few more minutes of high-speed flying, the space craft started to lower itself through the clouds again. Santa started to speed up the reindeer, getting as close as possible and as the clouds parted Frankie recognised where they were.

"This is Washington D.C." Frankie exclaimed. "Are they going after the president?"

"I think they might already have her." Santa said as he pointed to the grassy area in front of the White House. There were at least twenty alien spaceships dotted around the front of the building.

The ship they were following lowered itself into the middle of the cluster as Santa flew overhead.

"Where are we going?" Frankie demanded.

"It's too dangerous to leave the sleigh this close to all those ships." Santa explained.

"If they have captured the President then we should land on the White House. After all, it's one of the most guarded places on Earth, and it's where she lives, they might need our help." Frankie suggested.

"I like it." Santa pulled on the control reins and the eight reindeer took a sharp left, turning towards the large, white mansion.

Frankie started to panic when he saw the snipers and armed soldiers on the roof. This would have been a tough night for them. They were trying to stop an alien threat that could walk through walls. The bullets they fired would have passed straight through the aliens, they were impossible to stop.

Frankie could almost see the relief on their faces when they saw Santa's sleigh. It was obvious how happy they were as they waved Santa down and cleared a space on the roof.

"What's the situation?" Santa asked a young corporal who ran up to him the moment they landed.

"A new alien has just breached the Oval Office. The president was in the panic room but we heard a lot of commotion and then we lost communication." Said the man wearing enough body armour to stop a train.

"Don't worry, I'm here to help." Santa said in his usual, calm voice as he helped Frankie out of the sleigh.

"Sir, the boy, he cannot go inside." The officer said, trying to sound brave in front of the giant, bearded man.

"Michael, this is a moment that the world will never forget, and Frankie is going to play a key role, so he must go inside." Santa explained to the man who looked at Frankie and back at Santa.

"It's protocol. I cannot grant him access." Michael said as he shifted in his heavy, bulletproof vest.

"Michael, remember when you were ten years old. That action figure you wanted, the one from Star Wars. You put your faith in me then, and I delivered. Have faith in me now." Santa insisted.

They both looked at Frankie who stood there, holding his lightsabre that suddenly lit up in the dark. Although he was no longer wearing his cloak, he still reminded Michael of the Jedi heroes of his childhood.

The pleasure on Michaels's face was difficult to see underneath the helmet and face mask but the twinkle in his eyes made it obvious that Santa had convinced him.

"I suppose I couldn't stop you even if I wanted too. We couldn't stop the aliens, they just walked through the walls. Good luck Santa, and good luck to you, young man!" Michael said to Frankie as they walked across the roof of the most secure building in the world.

"Thank you." Santa said as he dismissed the guard.

"Good luck Santa!" He replied.

"Did you hear what he said? A *new* alien broke into the Oval Office." Frankie said as he walked along the rooftop next to Santa.

"Sounds like the queen to me. Are you ready to save the president?" Santa asked as he turned to Frankie.

"Sure, but how do we get in?" Frankie asked.

"The same way I get into every house, through the chimney. If I remember correctly that one goes into the guest bedrooms, that one down to the kitchen and this is the one that goes into the Oval Office." Santa said as they stood next to the stacks of chimneys.

"Okay." Frankie said, his voice quivering as he tightened his grip on the lightsabre.

"Are you ready?" Santa asked but didn't give Frankie time to answer, one moment they were on top of the roof in the cold winter air, the next, they were standing in front of the fireplace in the Oval Office.

As Frankie's eyesight readjusted he could see the famous room. It was empty and dark. All the doors had been sealed on the inside with some type of slime, obviously by the aliens.

"They must be close, but it's difficult to see." Frankie said, squinting in the darkness.

"Why don't you use your extendable glowing light stick?" Santa asked.

"You mean my lightsabre?" Frankie held up the plastic sword and extended it. "It's not the brightest."

"I gave you that as a present last Christmas, so it's not a lightsabre, it's an extendable glowing light stick, otherwise Disney will try and sue me. Also, turn it on, let's see how bright it really is." Santa encouraged him to press the button.

As he did the plastic turned to metal in his hand, the green, extendable tube dissolved away and Frankie found himself holding a real, working lightsabre. He pressed the button again and a green beam of pure energy appeared, casting the room in a soft light.

"Cool! Thank you Santa!" Frankie said as he waved the green, glowing stick around in the air, listening to the buzz as it moved. "I do feel this is a bit too dangerous for me."

"Touch it against the desk." Santa insisted.

"That's the president's desk! If I destroy it, I'll spend the rest of my life in jail!" Frankie argued.

"Just trust me." Santa urged.

Nervously Frankie lowered the glowing light onto the desk, expecting to see it burn through like in the movies.

"It's not doing anything. It's just light." Frankie observed as the beam wrapped around the edge of the desk.

"It's completely safe." Santa reassured him as he put his gloved hand through the blade and cast a shadow on the far wall. "Don't forget, I make toys not weapons!"

"Do that again with your hand." Frankie commanded.

The abruptness of the order took Santa by surprise, but he did as he was told. Frankie's gaze never left the wall opposite as the shadow was once again cast over it.

"There, it's a fake wall, you can tell because it doesn't quite line up, the shadows are all wrong."

He was right, as the shadow cast over a bookcase that was built into the wall, the surrounding area dimmed but the bookcase stayed the same colour, it looked like a bad video game as the obvious secret passage lit up in front of them.

"Hold on." Santa said as he reached into his sack.

He started pulling out a long fishing pole from the sack. It was too long to fit in the bag but as Frankie watched, Santa just kept on pulling. This must have been where magicians got their ideas for magic tricks from.

Santa held up the pole that was easily three times Frankie's height, then began to swing it around the room.

Smash

"Santa, that's probably a very expensive painting you have just knocked on the floor." Frankie commented as he waved the glowing lightsabre behind them to get a better look.

"Relax, it's only a copy." Santa said as he started to poke the wall around the bookcase carefully.

With every prod the bookcase shimmered. Growing in confidence he pushed the rod through the fake books, like they weren't really there.

"It's a hologram." Santa whispered to Frankie.

"Cool." Frankie replied.

"Yeah, we weren't planning on releasing this technology for another five Christmases. Watch this."

With a shake of his wrist, glitter started to weave its way out of Santa's sleeve, along his glove and up the fishing pole towards the wall. As the magic dust met the hologram a bright light engulfed the room, temporarily blinding Frankie. He turned away to shield his eyes and when he looked back, he could see a little, secret room where the bookcase once stood.

The room was surrounded in metal sheets, with dim lights all around. It was the President's personal bombproof panic room and inside, the familiar face of the President of the United States was smiling back, happy to see Santa.

"Nice to see you again, ma'am." Santa said. "We'll get you free in a moment."

Then everyone's eyes gazed up to the creature that was holding her hostage. A large, four-armed, four-legged monster, much scarier than the clumsy aliens they had previously met. The queen.

In one, long green arm she held the President, in another, she held Chloe.

Chapter 18

"Have you found anything?" Sophia asked as they investigated the room Walt Disney had designed for himself.

"There is nothing here. It's just a hotel room, everything has changed since it was built." Kevin said as he pointed out at the modern TV, mini bar and hotel welcome pack.

"There has to be something." Sophia argued, refusing to give up.

"Let's just stop and think. If you were Walt Disney, where would you hide something so that it wouldn't be found?" Marko pondered as he looked inside draws and cupboards.

"I don't think there is anything special here to begin with." Kevin argued. "We are wasting our time."

"Wait a minute, this is Cinderella's Castle, right? And in the movie she talked to mice." Sophia trailed off as she ran into the bedroom.

Kevin, Marko, Tony and Jade all looked at each other, confused at where she was heading with this thought, but they followed her, eager to see what she was thinking.

"Yeah, the film had mice that could talk." Marko said, remembering the film from his childhood.

"I remember seeing a little hole in the wall, a mouse hole." She leant down and looked underneath a dressing table. "Down here. A little mouse hole."

"Kevin, grab the table, let's move it out." Marko instructed and the two boys picked up an end each, careful not to drop the mirror that sat on top.

Sophia was right, a little mouse hole, just like in a cartoon movie.

"Well done, but now what?" Kevin asked. "It's probably been there for years, added by the original builders as a joke."

"I don't know. I just thought it might be a sign or something." Sophia sighed.

"Let me take a look." Marko crouched on the floor and tried to investigate the little hole. "It's dark but there might be something back here. Hold on."

He leant back, put his hand into the hole and pulled on the wall. Nothing. He switched positions and tried again. Still nothing.

"Wait!" Kevin yelled in excitement. "Something moved. Pull it upwards."

Marko did as instructed. Instead of pulling like a normal door, he stood above the little hole and pulled up, similar to the way he would open a garage door. After a bit of effort, it started to come loose, and the wall glided up into the roof.

"A hidden room!" Sophia shouted as she ran through the gap in the wall.

Marko had revealed a small closet, filled with drawings and photographs. Sophia pulled on a light switch and the room lit up with fairy lights all around. It was a magical little room filled with memories of the days when Walt was alive.

"This is Walt Disney with Santa!" Kevin said as he grabbed a photo that was hanging on the wall.

"Really?" Marko examined the pictures and found it to be true. "Wow, I bet there are a lot of good stories about this!"

"Look at all these original drawings, they must be worth a fortune." Kevin said as he looked up at the incomplete designs for characters. There were hundreds of pieces of paper pegged to string crisscrossing the little room.

"I am not so sure they would be worth anything. They are all unfinished." Marko said as he pointed out that many were missing eyes, arms and hands. There was a donkey with only three and a half legs, a kangaroo without a tail and most disturbing was a fish with only a head.

"It looks like this is where Walt wanted to create his characters." Sophia moved a pile of papers to reveal a little writing desk with an incomplete drawing on it and a pen left ready to resume.

"This all looks a little too fake." Kevin said as he admired the little room. "I thought Walt Disney died before this place was even built?"

"That's a good point." Sophia said as she took a seat at the desk.

"I agree, it seems like this has been set up for something. I don't know why, but I think you should finish off the drawing on the desk." Marko said as he looked around the room for clues.

None of the teenagers spotted the two elves who were smiling and waiting expectantly at the entrance to the door. They knew what was coming.

"You want me to finish off the drawing on the table?" Sophia asked, making sure she heard correctly.

"Yes, it can't be me, I can't draw." Marko explained.

"And I am colour-blind." Kevin reminded her.

"That's no excuse!" Sophia argued.

"That's my excuse, besides, you're the one in the chair." He replied.

"Really? Okay then." Sophia agreed. She picked up the pen and started to finish off the drawing that had already been started. "It seems to be some sort of wolf, but it's missing its tail. I can add one."

Sophia leaned forward and began to draw, carefully sketching over the pencil markings with Walt's pen.

"There, done. This pen draws superbly by the way! Now what?" She asked as she held up the piece of paper for the room to see.

"Look for yourself!" Marko said, staring at the paper as his eyes bulged.

"What do you mean?" Sophia turned the paper towards her but dropped it the moment she saw the other side. The picture was moving, the wolf had come alive.

On the floor the piece of paper started to fold and bend, then it grew in size. A few moments later a three-dimensional cartoon wolf stood in between Sophia and the rest of the group.

She was trapped in the cupboard behind the paper wolf, but she was safe for the moment, the wolf had its focus on the two boys and two elves that were slowly backing away out of the door.

The wolf snarled, at them. Then choked and finally coughed up a ball of paper which it spat out onto the floor.

"Sorry about that, nice to meet you?" The wolf said in a posh accent.

Kevin feinted.

"You can talk!" Marko shouted as the two elves ran and caught Kevin's body before he hit the ground.

"Of course I can talk." The wolf confirmed. "Why do you look so scared?"

Marko stood frozen, staring at the white wolf, unresponsive. It wasn't every day that you are faced with a talking cartoon character, so it takes a while to figure out how to behave around it.

The wolf stared at itself in a nearby mirror, checking over its new body to see what Marko was looking at. As it did, it saw Sophia hiding behind the desk. Seeing the girl made the wolf jump in fear.

"Sorry, you scared me, I didn't know you were there!" The wolf said.

"I'm sorry?" Sophia said, unsure of who or what she was talking to. "What are you?"

"I'm your creation. I could ask you the same thing." The wolf argued.

"What happened?" Kevin asked as he started to wake up again only to see the wolf talking to Sophia. He fainted once again.

"I think I know what is happening." Tony started to explain. "That pen, Santa must have given it to Walt Disney to help him spread joy in the world."

"You mean it's magical?" Sophia asked as she held up the little black felt tip.

"Yes, and obviously it brings whatever you draw to life." Tony confirmed.

"I don't want to sound ungrateful, but don't we have bigger things to worry about right now?" Marko asked. "The world is being taken over by aliens!"

On cue, a rumbling could be heard out near the stairs, then three aliens barged into the room. They were holding their devices and shot at Marko. A green laser beam flew past his ear, hitting the window behind.

The explosion was loud, louder than anything these teenagers had ever heard, and they had been to some pretty loud concerts.

The explosion blew a hole in the side of the castle, revealing the room to the world. Luckily it missed Marko, but the alien was not taking any chances, it was already lining up another shot.

The wolf saw this new threat and reacted faster than anyone else. It bounded across the room and bit the alien's hand clean off. As the wolf turned for another attack the alien disappeared in a green mist. Jumping through this strange cloud the angry wolf turned its attention on the other two green spacemen.

Within seconds they were green mist too as the wolf bit into them. It was an unfair battle, the wolf could move so much faster than the aliens. After the victory it bounded over to the new hole in the wall and howled at the moon.

"Sorry, I just couldn't control myself." The wolf said, embarrassed at the howling. "There are even more green men out here you know."

Everyone ran over to the edge of the room, to the new hole where they could see dozens of aliens starting to climb up the castle walls like ants.

"Quickly, finish more of the drawings, the cartoons can fight the aliens." Marko suggested as he pulled on an unfinished drawing from the ceiling.

"What's going on?" Kevin asked again as he woke up.

"No time to explain, find the scariest drawings and give them to Sophia to finish off." Marko ordered as Tony helped Kevin back to his feet.

"Sure thing." Kevin said as his eyes caught sight of the wolf hanging out of the huge hole in the wall.

"How about a boxing kangaroo?" Marko asked as he picked one of the pictures hanging above him.

"Great!" Sophia took it and quickly drew its missing foot. She threw it on the floor and just like before, the paper twisted and wrapped itself up until a large, boxing glove wearing, cartoon kangaroo stood before them.

"G'Day" The kangaroo said.

"Hi, no time to explain but the world is being attacked by aliens and we need you to fight." Marko explained.

"No worries." The kangaroo said as it bounced over to the wolf that was busy nipping and biting the army of aliens trying to get into the room.

"Here's a chicken." Kevin said as he handed Marko a picture of an unfinished, weak looking creature.

"Really? A chicken? Can't we find something better?" Marko argued.

"Fine then, how about a bear?" Kevin gave the piece of paper to Sophia who repeated the ritual, finishing off its paw. Moments later a roughly drawn bear appeared in front of them.

This went on for a few minutes, all kinds of animals, lions, spiders and penguins all poured out of the castle, pushing back the alien army.

The green men tried to fight back, firing their lasers at the cartoon creatures, sometimes they hit them, creating an explosion of confetti, but they were terrible at aiming and missed most of the time.

Instead, eagles picked up the green men and dropped them into open mouths of crocodiles, snakes would curl around them, holding them tight until they turned to smoke, all while a group of cartoon cowboys on horses galloped around shooting every enemy in sight.

Then it happened, Sophia finished off the spines on a dragons back and dropped the drawing to the floor.

The noise was incredible as the building fell apart around them. As it grew, the paper dragon pushed its way through the ceiling, out of the walls and through the windows until it was free, leaving behind a destroyed castle.

A couple of flaps from its huge wings and it was off chasing down the flying spacecraft that were already trying to get away.

Marko watched as the dragon landed and blew flames at a crowd of aliens, turning them all to green mist. Unfortunately, the dragon was made of paper, and the flames also set fire to its own nose.

In a blind panic the dragon ran through the park, it's face on fire, knocking over rides and stepping on both cartoons and aliens alike until it found the lake near the castle.

The giant dragon dunked its head into the water and put out the flames. It was a strange sight, a dragon with a soggy face.

From his viewpoint at the top of a destroyed castle Marko could see the entire park. It was full of cartoon creations fighting against aliens.

"Help!" The screams came from behind him, it was Sophia! She was dangling from the edge of the castle in the wreckage left from the huge dragon.

"I got you sis!" Marko screamed as he ran and perched over the edge trying to figure out how to reach his sister. She was just out of reach and hanging from a wooden beam above a huge drop.

"I need some rope!" Marko shouted.

"Here you go." Tony took off his hat and started to pull out long lengths of tinsel.

"Here, grab this!" Marko threw it down and after a bit of fumbling Sophia finally grabbed it. "We are going to pull you up, ready?"

Marko looked behind to see Kevin holding the tinsel, behind him, two elves, ready to safe Sophia.

"Pull!" Kevin shouted.

With effort they managed to pull Sophia back into the safety of the castle.

"It's a good job there isn't a mirror around here. You look like you haven't showered in a month!" Marko jested.

"Shut up, now is not the time." Sophia scowled at her brother. "Where did that pen go?"

"It's over there, I'll get it." Kevin said as he ran across to the other side of the room where the pen lay on the floor.

He bent down to pick it up but instead, his foot clumsily kicked it towards the edge.

"Oops." Kevin said, smiling back at the others.

"Kevin, now is not the time to be clumsy." Marko said.

"Don't worry, I've got it." Kevin jogged over to the pen and once again, as he bent over, his foot met the pen and he kicked it, straight out of the room, through the new hole in the wall and down into the water below.

Everyone ran over just in time to see it plop into the lake under the castle.

"Well, I guess that's the end of the cartoon army." Marko said.

"Sorry guys." Kevin apologised as he stared into the dark theme park below.

"Don't worry about it, I don't think we need any more anyway, look." Sophia nudged Kevin to look out into the park.

Everywhere Kevin looked there were cartoons chasing aliens, running them down and turning them to mist. There were hundreds of aliens, but they didn't stand a chance against the magical creatures.

"I have to get a picture of this." Marko said as he got out his phone.

He lined up the photo, trying to get as many cartoons in as possible. It was nearly perfect, then, he nearly dropped the phone as a new image appeared.

It was Frankie, he was calling.

Chapter 19

"Chloe!" Frankie shouted as soon as he saw his friend. He started to run forward but stopped as the new, much bigger and scarier alien held a device next to Chloe's head.

"Take one more step and she'll be gone forever." The alien said.

This must have been the queen. She was at least eight-foot-tall, had four legs and four arms, was a darker green than the other aliens and her face was terrifying. She lacked the little antenna that the other aliens had, instead they were replaced with large horns. Frankie thought she looked just like a dark green devil.

The queen had one arm around Chloe's neck and another around the President, holding them both in headlocks. With her other two arms she held devices to their heads.

To her credit, the President looked very calm, but Frankie guessed she was trained to handle hostage situations like this, Choe looked a lot more worried.

"Hold on a moment." Santa pulled back on Frankie's shoulders, stopping him from attacking. "Let's just stay calm and figure this out."

"You are the keeper of the key?" The queen asked.

Frankie was just about to reply but Santa interrupted him.

"Yes, I am the keeper." Santa replied.

"Then where is the key." The alien demanded.

"Why do you want it?" Santa asked.

"Like hundreds of planets before, you will join my army and help conquer the galaxy!" The queen bellowed as Santa started to move his sack behind him, trying to hide it from the alien.

"We cannot do that." Santa said as he fiddled with the sack.

"What is that you are hiding behind your back?" The alien asked as she tried to peer behind him. "Is that the key?"

The queen started to sweat green blobs of slime that she shook off, dripping onto the floor. These slime puddles started to move, to join, moving and flowing to form three aliens that stood in front of her.

"It's behind his back, the sack! Get it!" The queen hissed. The aliens jumped towards Santa.

He stepped to one side and nimbly dodged their attack like he was a ballerina. He had been coughing and wheezing all night but now he moved with the ease of a yoga expert. The aliens landed in a pile but quickly got back up to their feet.

"Frankie. Use the sword!" Santa ordered.

"Use the force?" Frankie misheard. He could smell something burning, then he noticed it. The beam on his lightsabre was slowly toasting a nearby stack of papers. It was no longer just a torch.

He quickly jabbed and swung at the nearest alien who vanished upon contact with the green laser sword. The other two aliens, upon seeing this, quickly jumped out of the way and scuttled upside down onto the ceiling.

"Is this what you want?" Santa balled up his sack and held it out. Both aliens jumped at him but missed, landing between him and Frankie who stood ready to attack if they got close enough.

"Is this what you want?" Santa asked again, throwing the scrunched-up sack from one hand to the other. The aliens watched, like dogs, as the ball moved.

"Fetch!" Santa shouted as he pretended to throw. The little aliens started to chase it, exactly like dogs. They looked confused when they didn't see it land, but then bounced back to Santa when they saw it, still in his hands.

"Fetch!" This time Santa pretended to throw it over their heads. They turned and ran forward, straight into the glowing stick in Frankie's hand. Then they were gone, turned to green mist.

"Now it's my turn." Santa unrolled the sack, reached inside and pulled out two elves who were holding cans of something. "Get her!"

The two elves shook their cans as they ran towards the queen. They pointed and unleashed a mountain of silly string straight into her green face. She wiped the strange foam from her eyes and, in doing so, let go of Chloe who immediately ran over to Frankie for safety.

The elves then pulled out their next weapons, three bowling pins each. They each threw one at the queen's face. The pins flew through the office on a direct flight with her face, but, at the last minute she let go of the devices and caught the wooden skittles.

Two more bowling pins came straight at her again and this time she had to let go of the president to catch them.

"Mrs President, over here." Frankie whispered as the fancy lady crawled over and hid behind the desk with the two teenagers.

Finally, two more pins flew across the room and the queen threw two of the pins she was already holding up into the air to catch the new ones.

Moments later and the queen was busy juggling bowling pins. It would have been the strangest circus act ever, a four-armed creature juggling six objects, but she wasn't very good. The first one she dropped exploded in a cloud of pink dust. This made her drop the rest as the little cupboard was engulfed in smoke of different colours.

"Get her!" The two little elves shouted as they leapt into the smoke, expecting to find the alien, but instead landing hard on the ground.

"Santa!" One of the elves shouted in a panic. "She's escaping!"

The smoke started to clear and a portal could be seen at the back of the closet, the queen jumped through. A pair of giant Christmas trees stood in front of a grotto, in the middle of a shopping centre. Then the portal closed, and the room went quiet.

"Are you safe Mrs President?" Santa asked as he peered over the desk.

"I am fine, thank you." The lady replied as she started to dust herself down. "Thank you for saving me."

The room suddenly filled with secret service agents as the slime on the doors started to weaken. They came in holding guns and pointing them around the room. Frankie and Chloe instinctively held up their hands.

"All clear." One man said into his radio.

"Are you safe ma'am?" A guard asked as he ran to the President's side.

"Yes, thanks to these wonderful kids!" She replied as she pushed the armed man away to re-join Santa. "Is the key safe?"

"Always." Santa grinned.

"Where did the queen go?" Frankie asked as he got to his feet and held out his hand to help Chloe to hers.

"I know where there are two trees like that." The President said. "She went to the Mall of America."

"A mall?" Chloe asked as she tried to gesture with her arms. Something was stopping her, then she realised, she was still holding Frankie's hand. They quickly let go of each other and blushed. "Why would she go to a mall?"

"Who cares. If that's where she has gone, we have to chase her, catch her off guard." Frankie insisted.

"The Mall of America? Then that's where we will go!" Santa bellowed.

"Be careful." Michael, the man from the roof said. "It might be a trap."

"Don't worry young Michael. We'll be safe." Santa chuckled. "It's going to take more than an alien queen to get the better of me."

"Sure, you say that now, but you let them catch me!" Chloe jokingly cried.

"If she didn't catch you, we wouldn't have known where she was." Santa said, pretending like it was all part of his plan.

"Well, you have all our resources at your disposal if you need backup." The officer said.

"Backup?" Santa pondered the idea. "Backup doesn't sound too bad. Frankie, call in your friends, tell them the queen is at the Mall of America!"

"Will do." Frankie agreed, reaching for his phone.

"Marko. The queen is at... Wait, what is going on around you?" Frankie could see what looked like cartoon characters in the background chasing aliens through a theme park.

"Is that the President?" Marko asked as the President peered over Frankie's shoulder, trying to see the screen.

"No time to explain. The queen is at the Mall of America. We need to get there now!" Frankie said.

"Will do!" Marko said as he started to hang up. Just before the connection went dead Frankie heard Sophia in the background.

"Mall of America? Are we going shopping?"

Chapter 20

The journey from Washington D.C. to the Mall of America took seconds in Santa's sleigh and it wasn't long enough for Chloe to truly say how thankful she was to Santa and Frankie for rescuing her.

"You're safe now!" Frankie reassured her as they hovered above the huge mall.

"I don't really remember much of it. I know I was standing in front of the Titanic staircase in Vegas, then the next thing I know, I am being held with the President, waiting for you to arrive." Chloe explained.

"Well, it should be me who is thanking you, after all, the aliens that shot you were after me, you sacrificed yourself." Frankie reminded her.

"I don't remember that. I suppose we could call it even then?" She suggested.

"Sounds good to me." Frankie agreed.

The car parks were full, which was usual for this time of year, but there weren't any cars, just giant spaceships sprawled across the roads, bridges and roofs. There were round, silver UFO's everywhere and Santa was struggling to find somewhere safe to land.

"There are just no good parking spots." Santa complained after the third flyover, then he pressed a button on the sleigh, a button Frankie was sure wasn't there five minutes ago. "Time to call in the cavalry."

Over in the distance a large blue glow was rising over the horizon. Frankie had to check the time on his phone, it was too early for sunrise, and it was blue.

Whatever it was approached quickly, covering the vast distances in seconds and then Frankie saw them. It was elves, hundreds of them, all flying on the back of reindeer and leaving a blue streak of energy behind.

Within minutes the carpark below was full. The little elves were pulling huge lengths of glittering tinsel out of their hats and attaching it to the legs of the alien spaceships. After all the spaceships were attached the elves whispered something into the reindeer's ears and then, woosh!

The reindeer started running, taking off into the sky, with the spaceships bouncing behind them. They rose into the air and pulled the spacecraft along, far away from the mall.

"Now we can land." Santa chuckled to himself as he waved to the elves that had stayed behind to create a landing area for him.

The sleigh landed perfectly on the rooftop and as they jumped out, a door opened revealing Marko, Sophia and Kevin.

"Guys!" Frankie and Chloe both shouted as they ran over. Chloe tried to give Sophia a hug but quickly backed away when she saw the slime-covered girl.

"Don't ask!" Sophia moaned.

Chloe noticed the mayhem behind the door before it closed, and a look of puzzlement came over her.

"Was that a cartoon dragon?" She asked as she peered around to get a better view.

"Yeah, we'll explain later." Marko said as everyone turned to face Santa, reunited at last.

"Tony, Jade, you're in charge out here. Make sure no aliens leave." Santa ordered his little elves. "We have the queen trapped inside!"

"What should we do?" Frankie asked as he reached for his lightsabre.

"We are heading inside. We are going queen hunting. She thinks she can come to this planet and ruin Christmas. We are going to teach her that Christmas is a time for giving, not stealing, and we are going to give her a lesson she will not forget!" Santa spoke in a confident tone that spurred everybody into life.

Everyone let out a cheer, Christmas music started to thunder into the sky and the little elves jumped on the back of reindeer and took to the skies, ready to fight off any UFO's that came to save their queen.

Santa held the door open and everyone started to creep down the stairwell and into the mall. The Christmas music slowly faded away behind them.

Now it was quiet. Really quiet. Malls are noisy places, they are designed that way, to make people feel surrounded and happy. This was different, an empty mall is creepy, and it put everyone on edge, especially when the occasional explosion could be heard from the elves fighting the aliens outside.

"We saw the Christmas trees when the queen escaped. The President told us to come here to find her." Frankie explained.

"You met the president?" Sophia asked.

"Chloe had an up-close and personal encounter." Frankie reminded her.

"Yes, but let's focus on what we are here to do, I'll tell you the story later." Chloe insisted.

"Here, this is where we need to go." Kevin said as he stood in front of the mall map.

"If we head down here, take a left at the Makeup Shack." Marko traced the route and everyone stopped to look at Sophia at the sound of makeup.

"What?" Sophia asked. "Look at me, I am covered in slime and dust, do you think I care about makeup right now?"

"Fair enough." Chloe said, picking up where Marko left off. "Then we could cut across the indoor theme park."

"Please! No more theme parks." Kevin moaned.

"Okay then, we go around the theme park and towards the Christmas trees where the queen was last seen." Chloe said.

"I'm ready." Marko said as he pulled out his gun and loaded a foam bullet.

"Where did you get that from?" Santa asked, already knowing the answer. "I'm going to have words with Tony and Jade!"

"Oh yeah, we aren't supposed to show you our weapons." Marko remembered.

"Our weapons?" Santa asked, turning to Sophia and Kevin who pulled out the bag of beads and bat, ready for Santa to take them away.

"I suppose given the situation a few magical items might be useful." Santa admitted. "Frankie, you still have your light sword."

Frankie held up the metal object in his hand. He pressed the button and it buzzed into life.

"Wow! A real lightsabre!" Kevin gasped as the green light glowed across his face.

"It's a glowing light stick." Frankie corrected him as he smiled as Santa.

"Now we just need something for Chloe." Santa said, reaching into his sack. "Let me think…"

Chloe leaned forward in anticipation and watched as Santa pulled out a guitar.

"Wow! A Gibson Firebird!" She said excitedly as she threw the strap over her head.

"It was on your Christmas list this year, normally I don't like giving gifts out early but this year I will make an exception." Santa explained.

"I love it, but what can a guitar do against aliens?" She asked.

"When you play it in front of them, you will know." Santa said. "Right, onwards!"

Everyone stepped into the long mall corridor, surrounded by stores on all sides. They held their weapons ready for any aliens that tried to stop them.

"Over here." Frankie whispered as he spotted something through a store window.

It was a hairdresser. Inside was a small group of aliens, one was sat in a chair while another stood behind and adjusted its antenna. Another two sat with their heads inside large hairdryers, chatting away while reading magazines that they held upside down.

The whole image didn't make any sense until another alien came into view carrying what looked like an alien camera. This is the conclusion that Frankie had because, like a photographer, he moved around the shop while the aliens posed for photographs.

"Are we sure this is real?" Chloe asked as they peeked into the shop.

"I know, this isn't the alien threat we were promised in the movies." Kevin agreed. "Not that I am complaining."

"I know, they are so stupid, they haven't even turned the hairdryers on." Sophia added.

They all backed away from the window slowly, trying not to get the aliens attention. Chloe was the last to move but, as she turned, the neck of the guitar hit against the glass window causing the faintest of taps.

Instantly the aliens all turned to see the five teenagers backing away from the window. They ran towards the large glass door, angry that their photo session had been disturbed.

The first one didn't notice the glass and smacked into it, leaving a slimy imprint. The second and third collided with the first and they all slid onto the ground in a slump. The next alien jumped up, over its alien friends and fired a laser beam at the glass door. A portal appeared and the remaining two aliens passed straight through, landing in front of the gang.

"Chloe, now!" Santa urged, looking at her guitar.

Chloe reached down and started to strum out a guitar solo. She was really good, all the lessons for ten years were worth it, and her solo sounded great, too good, like it was being amped up by an unknown set of speakers somewhere.

The aliens didn't think it sounded good at all. They all held their hands to the ends of their antennae, covering them like humans would cover their ears, and wincing at the sound.

"Marko. Shoot them." Santa said as he got excited, seeing the aliens in pain from the guitar sound.

Marko took aim with the toy gun and fired two bullets straight into the alien's mouths. As soon as they hit, the aliens disappeared into green smoke that was quickly sucked up into a nearby air conditioning unit.

Sophia put her hand through the portal in the glass door and sprinkled the heap of aliens with her beads, causing them to turn into green smoke and disappear too. She removed her hand just as the portal closed.

"I just thought they might wake up." Sophia said as the group watched her.

"Good thinking." Santa confirmed. "Let's keep going."

Further along the hallway, three and a half shops along, an explosion of glass and tinsel flew out and across their path.

As the dust settled a man wearing a red suit came running out holding onto a big sack. A fake white beard was wrapped around his neck, facing the wrong way.

Moments later this new Santa was on the floor again as aliens leapt from the store and held him down on the ground.

Everybody in the group looked at each other, prepared their weapons and ran towards the little green men.

Marko was first with a hit from his gun, causing one of the dozen aliens to disappear. Next, Sophia threw a handful of beads at the group causing three more to vanish but also hitting the new Santa in the eye.

"Careful." Kevin said as he ran past Sophia and leapt at the aliens with his bat in hand. Frankie was alongside him with his lightsabre and together they made a sweep of the aliens, taking them by surprise and turning five more into smoke.

There were only three left and they started to run. They made it a few yards away before stopping, paralysed in place. Chloe had started another awesome guitar solo causing them to freeze up. Marko took aim and hit each one on the back of the head.

"Thank you." The slim Santa panted as he climbed to his feet. "I have been trapped in there for hours!"

"Don't worry Clive, your safe now." Santa said.

"Your beard… your suit… You're…" Clive stuttered as he looked up at the big man wearing the same red suit as him.

"I know! Isn't it embarrassing when two people turn up at a party wearing the same thing!" Santa chuckled as he compared his red coat to Clive's. Then he reached into his sack and pulled out an elf. "Don't worry, Christine here will get you to safety."

The little elf with a pink jumper nodded grabbed Clive's hand, helping him to his feet. Together the elf and the confused mall Santa walked over to an emergency exit.

"Clive is a good man. He has been standing in for me here for twenty years and I never visit him. These aliens are really starting to get on my nerves." Santa said, focusing his face and the first sign of anger growing on the usually jolly man.

Slowly the group made their way past many of the empty stores, gazing inside, not sure what to expect. Within one of the children's stores a television had been left on and three aliens were hypnotised by the colourful characters. They stood staring at the screen, singing the songs that had been on repeat for hours. The group decided to ignore them.

"I think we are getting closer." Chloe whispered as she signalled that there were aliens up ahead.

Frankie realised they were on the second level of the mall as a large, four storey atrium opened in front of him. In front of them stood two large trees that came from the floor below and towered high above them.

The trees surrounded a stage with a large screen and a Santa's grotto in the middle.

"Look." Kevin pointed as the queen made her way across the stage and into the little hut where Santa would normally be sitting.

"It's the queen!" Chloe squealed, then ducked on the floor to calm herself. She did not have good memories of that creature and it showed.

"It's fine, your safe with all of us." Frankie sat next to her and offered his hand to pull her back to her feet. She looked up and saw his determination and confidence.

"Let's do this!" Chloe said with conviction.

"If I can get close, I can stop her." Santa explained.

"Then we need to get you inside that grotto." Chloe stated, determined to get even with the queen.

As the group looked down on the stage there were aliens everywhere, marching around and guarding the queen inside the little gingerbread house.

"How are we going to get through all those aliens without getting zapped?" Sophia asked. "There are too many of them!"

"We need a distraction." Marko suggested.

"I have a plan." Frankie said as he pointed at the main crowd of aliens. "I will get the aliens attention, make them chase me through that far door and upstairs. Sophia, you can stand in that balcony, ready with the beads. As I run underneath, pour everything you have onto the aliens. Chloe, be ready with the guitar if they get too close. Marko, you and Kevin go with Santa, sneak in from behind and clear any remaining aliens. Santa, you get in that little house and do what you need to do."

"Sounds like a good plan!" Marko agreed.

"Are you sure you want to be the one who gets their attention?" Chloe asked.

"It's my plan, I couldn't ask anyone else to do it, it's time someone stood up to these creatures. I'll head down the far stairs, Marko, Kevin and Santa, you use the elevator behind the stage, Sophia and Chloe, stand above me and get ready." Frankie ordered as everyone split up and headed to their locations. It was time to get even with these aliens!

Chapter 21

The area in front of the stage was covered in little green men, all wandering around, minding their own business. Some of them were zooming around on two wheeled hoverboards they had stolen, while others were wearing clothes they had taken from mannequins.

The weirdest sight was the alien who was handing out cups of coffee it had made from the nearby bistro. It was funny watching the aliens, who had never tasted coffee before. They eagerly took the cup, put it to their lips then instantly spat it out. Clearly coffee was not for everyone.

They were minding their own business when a door on the far side flung open, grabbing all their attention. Christmas music started to boom, and a fog machine filled the floor with mist.

"Now that's how you get the aliens attention!" Marko said as they waited for the distraction.

In the foggy darkness an outline of a teenage boy was visible. It was Frankie, and as his green lightsabre grew and lit him, highlighting the anger on his face. He looked up, noticed the aliens starting to approach him, and ran to the staircase behind.

The aliens quickly followed and they nearly made it to the door, but Sophia started a waterfall of beads from above. Some disappeared instantly, others slipped on the bead and vanished in mid-air as they fell.

The plan was working, nearly half the aliens had already gone and the rest were chasing Frankie.

On the other side of the stage Marko, Kevin and Santa used the distraction to make their way out of the elevator and towards the queen's hiding place, taking shots at aliens along the way.

Frankie made it to the stairs and looked behind him, some of the aliens had made it through the bead river and were closing the gap. He scrambled up, slipping on a few of the steps but making it up to the top where Chloe was waiting with her guitar.

"Marko, over to your right." Kevin shouted as they climbed onto the stage. He shot several of the aliens with his toy gun.

"I need to reload." Marko shouted to Kevin who was busy helping Santa onto the stage. He looked up, saw two aliens approaching.

Kevin quickly grabbed a Christmas decoration off the nearby tree. Of all the things he could have picked, reindeer, stars, presents, he happened to grab two little trolls. He threw them up and hit them towards the approaching aliens.

As soon as the trolls hit their targets they came alive and started to run through the crowd, biting ankles, pulling antennae and turning the little green men to dust.

"Good choice!" Marko commented.

Sophia was busy throwing beads down onto the main crowd of aliens, she had cleared over a hundred but some were still getting through. All she had to do was keep them busy while Santa sneaked in behind.

"Chloe, ready?" Frankie shouted as he scrambled behind her, watching the aliens appear from the stairwell. "Now!"

Chloe started a bone chilling guitar solo. Santa must have done something magical because it sounded like it was playing through a huge speaker, like she was on stage at a festival.

As the aliens climbed the stairs they stopped to look at the guitar. Then they continued their approach.

"It's no good!" Frankie said, stopping Chloe in the middle of her performance. "They are wearing woolly hats! They can't hear the guitar."

It was true, the aliens were now wearing little Christmas hat, hiding their antennae. The guitar sounds that had paralysed the previous aliens were no longer working.

Frankie grabbed Chloe as he ran past and together, they headed towards Sophia for protection.

"Marko, up there!" Kevin shouted as he smashed his bat into a couple of aliens that landed from the tree above.

The aliens were jumping onto the tree from the top floors of the mall, were climbing down and landing on the stage.

"I've got this. You get Santa inside." Marko shouted as he fired at the aliens overhead. Kevin and Santa ran across the stage, Kevin took a swing at the aliens that were guarding the entrance, turning them to green mist and allowing him to get into the little hut.

"Guy's this isn't working anymore." Sophia shouted as Frankie and Chloe finally joined her. Below, several aliens had put up umbrellas and now Sophia could no longer hit them as they ran underneath.

"We know!" Chloe replied as they backed up towards her, the alien army wearing bobble hats surrounding them, pushing them up against the railings.

Sophia turned and started to throw beads at the oncoming aliens, but it was no good, they also had umbrellas and used them as shields to protect themselves from Sophia's deadly beads.

"Be careful." Kevin said as they made their way through the dimly lit house. There was tinsel hanging from the ceiling and balloons floated everywhere, it would have been a great experience as a child, but as a teenage alien killer it made it impossible to see any green creatures hiding inside.

Finally, they found the main room.

"Follow my lead." Santa said as he walked in confidently and confronted the queen. She was sat in the chair used by Santa to bring joy to children.

"Get out of my chair!" Santa said as he strode across the room, his hand reaching inside his sack for something.

Kevin followed, saw the queen but also noticed six other aliens surrounding the door.

"Santa stop!" Kevin shouted, but it was too late. The jolly man stood on a bear rug in the middle of the room. The aliens pulled on ropes and a large net appeared from underneath, raising up and catching Santa. Trapping him in a giant net.

"Let go of him!" Kevin shouted as he started to swing his bat at the aliens that were holding onto the ropes. He missed with his first swing and by the time he had recovered it was too late. Another net appeared underneath him and caught him in mid-air too.

"So, your name is Santa?" The queen asked the man in the red suit who was hanging upside down in the giant net.

"You better let me go!" Santa argued as he struggled.

"You cannot escape this net, if you want to go free just tell me where the key is." The queen hissed as she got up from the seat and circled Santa, towering over him, at least twice his size.

"You can't have it!" Santa replied.

"If you don't want to tell me, I have ways to make you talk!" The queen picked up the net with one of her four arms and lifted Santa, like he was weightless.

"What about this one?" The little green men asked, pointing at Kevin.

"Stick him with the others. If I need them, I'll come back for them." The queen said as she spun Kevin in the air. Then she leapt out of the top of the house and climbed up the nearby Christmas tree like a spider, carrying Santa on her back.

"Look!" Chloe said, as the explosion from the roof of the grotto took their attention away from the aliens that surrounded them.

"That's the queen, and... is that Santa on her back?" Sophia asked.

"What have we done?" Frankie sobbed at the sight of Santa hanging helplessly from the back of the queen.

Another explosion overhead created a hole in the roof of the mall, the cool night air, floating in from outside, a night that had suddenly gone quiet, no elves fighting aliens, no reindeer flying, no Christmas music.

Frankie, Chloe and Sophia put their hands in the air and turned to face the stage. They could see Marko doing the same thing. He had run out of bullets and was surrounded by aliens. Then the door to Santa's grotto opened and three aliens were dragging Kevin out in a net. It was all over.

Chapter 22

Frankie nudged Marko who was starting to fidget. They were sat underneath the large net that had caught Kevin, unable to stand, surrounded by aliens who were waiting to hear orders from their queen. They had been like this for what seemed like an hour, although it was probably only ten minutes.

"If you are going to kill us, just do it already!" Sophia yelled.

"Not until we have the key, if Santa wont hand it over, maybe you will." One of the aliens said, prodding Sophia with a large candy cane decoration.

"We really screwed up guys." Marko said.

"Hey, don't give up yet." Kevin replied. "You didn't screw up, I did, I should have kept Santa safe, besides, Santa won't give away the secret."

"If he doesn't then they will torture us, either way, it doesn't look good." Marko commented.

"It was such an obvious trap to get Santa here. Their plan was obvious the moment they caught me. Using one of us as bait, showing us where the trap was. It was so obvious! I should have spotted it." Chloe said, annoyed at herself.

"What can we do? We can't fight back? They have our weapons and they outnumber us a hundred to one!" Marko pointed out.

"It was my plan, and it failed, if anyone is to blame its me." Frankie said. "But we can't give up. My sister is out there with the key and I need to protect her!"

"Well I'm not ready to give up either. There is no way I am staying here, smelling like a swamp!" Sophia said as another inflatable candy cane hit her on the head.

"Stop talking otherwise you'll be sorry!" An alien shouted, then spoke something into its device, talking to the queen about something. Then it stopped and turned its antennae towards the main entrance.

"Can you hear that?" Chloe asked.

"It sounds like Christmas music." Marko replied, unsure about what he was hearing. The music was growing louder, it was jingle bells and it was coming from the front of the mall.

The five of them turned to face the entrance as the doors blew open and reindeer started to run into the mall. Dozens of reindeer with dozens of Santa's riding on their backs! The Santa's came in all ages, sizes, races and genders. They were holding pirate swords, lightsabres, hockey sticks and anything else they could get their hands on.

As the reindeer ran through the crowd of aliens, they speared the little green men with their antlers, causing popping sounds all around as they turned into green smoke.

The aliens didn't know what to do. They tried firing their lasers at the wild beasts, but they were too slow and by the time anyone could figure out what was going on, half the aliens had disappeared.

There was only one thing left to do, run away, down every escape route, on every floor of the mall, away from the new army of Santa's.

"Need a hand?" One of the Santa's said as he pulled the net off the teenagers.

It was Clive, the Santa they had saved a few hours ago. He was on the back of a red nosed reindeer and had clearly organised everything going on around them.

"Clive! How did you do this?" Frankie asked, looking around at the dozens of Santa's that had appeared.

"I heard the aliens talking about the trap they were setting for Santa. When you guys freed me you looked like you knew what you were doing but I called in some help, just in case!" Clive explained.

"Thank you!" Sophia said. "But I have some bad news, they caught Santa."

"I know, I saw them carrying him into one of the spaceships while we were gathering in the car park." Clive explained. "Then they took off before we could save him. I tried, but this reindeer doesn't fly."

"So how do we save Santa?" Kevin asked.

"I have an idea." Chloe suggested. "But we need to capture one of the aliens first."

As soon as Clive lifted the net the five of them ran to grab their weapons and prepare to take on the aliens once again.

"Let's go get some aliens!" Frankie said as he pressed the button on his lightsabre. The plastic tube expanded and lit up a dim green but it didn't hum, it wasn't bright and it was still plastic. "What? It's not real anymore!"

"My sack is out of beads." Sophia said as she turned the little bag inside out.

"This guitar, it sounds normal again." Chloe said as she played a little tune that was hard to hear amongst the chaos around.

"Hold on." Kevin picked up his bat. Took a decoration off a nearby tree and pointed to the star on top. He threw it up, swung and missed. The glass decoration hit the ground and smashed.

"So, we have no more magic. That won't stop us." Marko said confidently. "If Chloe needs an alien, we'll catch her an alien!"

The group made their way through the mall, hot on the tails of the Santa's riding the reindeer and catching up with the aliens who were now getting trapped down dead ends and wrong turns.

"If our weapons are no longer magical, how come the reindeer are still able to kill the aliens?" Kevin asked.

"Maybe reindeer have always been magical." Sophia suggested. "We just never gave them a chance."

"Here looks like a good place for a trap." Chloe interrupted.

Everyone stopped and entered a large clothing shop. It was dark inside, there was no power and luckily the alarm didn't sound when Marko and Kevin smashed the glass door.

"Chloe to Clive, we are in a store called…" Chloe looked at the name of the store and sighed. "Really? We couldn't pick a better store?"

"Hey, you picked the store." Marko reminded her.

"Clive we are in a store called 'Out Of This World'. Send them our way." Chloe ordered into her phone. Clive's face was on the screen, he smiled and nodded.

"Clive here, sending an alien your way."

Moments later the heavy stamping of reindeer could be heard. Sophia looked out of the store window and saw an alien being chased. It was on its own. Three Santa's chased it through the broken doorway and into the dark store. Then, when the reindeer couldn't fit through the door, they galloped away.

The alien let out a visible sigh of relief thinking it had escaped. It turned into the dark store and slowly started to walk towards the back. Past the first isle, then the next. On the third isle it looked left and jumped as a mannequin next to him stared back.

The little alien inspected the figure, realised that it was fake and started to chuckle to itself.

It crept past the next isle then once again jumped as a large bang came from the front of the store. Something had fallen over but the alien couldn't see what.

Finally, the little green man made it to the end of the shop. As the little figure walked past the till, it clanged and the draw opened. It was like being in a creepy movie, except it was the alien that was nervous.

Once again the alien jumped. This time it pulled out its device ready to shoot whatever was in the shadows. It was just the cash register. The little green man investigated the drawer. There was still money in it as the staff had run away in the middle of the day.

The alien didn't know what to do with the money, instead, he turned around, reached up and grabbed a door handle, pulling it open and into the storeroom behind. Where he thought he would be free.

As the door opened, the harsh light of the storeroom caused the big black eyes of the alien to turn brown for a moment. As its eyes became used to the light the green man saw a figure stood towering over him.

Zap!

The alien fired its device at the creature. A direct hit, but no screams or teleportation. Instead a plume of white cotton exploded from a giant teddy. The large, stuffed bear was a distraction while someone grabbed the aliens arm, and took away the device.

In one swift movement a giant net, made of tinsel, wrapped around the alien and pulled the little man into the air. The same way Kevin and Santa were caught.

Quickly Marko spun the alien around and Kevin hit the little, black device out of its hand with his bat.

"Well done, you caught me." The alien said sarcastically. The alien was calm, too calm, and it made Frankie feel uneasy, but this was his trap.

"Quickly grab the device." Kevin said.

Chloe picked it up and pointed it at the alien that was now hanging upside down, wrapped in tinsel.

"You cannot kill me! If you shoot me, I will return to my queen. Then I'll come back here for you!" The alien threatened as it chuckled to itself.

"We're counting on it!" Sophia said as she strapped her mobile phone to the alien.

"What's that for?" The little green man asked.

Nobody answered. Instead Chloe pressed a button on the device, firing a laser and disintegrating the phone along with the alien.

"Yes!" Marko yelled as the tinsel began to smoke where the alien once hung.

"Hold on, let me check." Chloe said as she tapped on her phone a few times. "We have a connection!"

"Where is the queen?" Frankie asked as he looked over Chloe's shoulder.

"Here, take a look." Chloe put the phone down. A little map appeared, and a dot glowed. "That's where the queen is!"

"Quickly get the location." Kevin shouted.

"Hold on, it's moving." Sophia said.

"Where is it heading?" Marko asked.

"Hold on, if we zoom out and triangulate the movement." Chloe picked up the phone and started to tap away. Then all the colour drained out of her face as she put the phone back down.

A little line traced from the queen all the way back to Frankie's house.

"They know where it is, we need to get back to Jess!" Frankie screamed. "I have to save her!"

He pulled out his phone and tried to call his mum.

"Wait!" Chloe said as she slapped the phone out of his hands. "We know where they are going, we can set a trap. And I know just how we can get there before they do!"

Chapter 23

"Let's hope this thing still knows how to fly." Frankie said as they jumped into the sleigh that was still parked on the roof of the huge mall.

"Thanks for all your help!" Sophia shouted to Clive who stood by the rooftop door waving them off and making sure no aliens followed them.

Frankie pulled on the reins of the deer and the sleigh rose into the air with a few bumps and jumps.

"Hold on, it's my first time flying!" Frankie said as he wrestled with the controls. "I just need to input the directions and then…"

The ground turned into a blur below them as they shot off and seconds later appeared over Frankie's house. The sun was starting to rise, casting a glowing red haze on the horizon. They didn't have much time. Frankie landed in the front garden and everyone jumped out onto the frozen ground.

"Marko, hide the sleigh in the garage." Frankie ordered as he rushed towards the front door. "Hurry, the queen will be here soon!"

Frankie quietly opened the front door, peeking inside to make sure the coast was clear. He barely put one foot on the polished wooden floor before the attack came.

Whatever it was, it wrapped its arms around his head and would not let go. It was heavier than an elf or an alien and seemed to be wearing some sort of cotton pyjamas.

"Jess, are you alright?" Sophia asked as she followed Frankie into the house. Jess let go of her brother's head and Frankie could once again see.

"We were having a great time; we had just decided to play another game of Twister and then all three of Santa's elves disappeared. I was about to go and wake mum up but then I heard you outside." Jess said frantically.

"Don't worry, we are here now, but some bad aliens are heading this way so it's important that you hide." Frankie said calmly.

Looking around he saw the house was a mess. Jess had clearly been having a lot of fun tonight with the elves but there was a lot of cleaning up to do.

"Why are the aliens coming here?" Jess asked.

"No time to explain. Here, hide in your sofa fort while we get the house ready." Frankie urged.

"I am scared." Jess said as her eyes started to flood with tears.

"It's going to be okay." He said as he stopped, knelt down and put his hand on her shoulder to comfort her. "The aliens have captured Santa but we are going to trap them and save the day. I need you to be brave one last time tonight and hide in your fort until this is all over. Do you think you can do that?"

"I think so, after all, I have your lucky clover to keep me safe." Jess said as she held out the small plant. Frankie had taped it to a piece of cardboard when he was younger and his mum had laminated it. It was torn and tattered from the years of carrying it around, but the actual leaves still looked like new.

"That's right, you hold on to that and it'll keep you safe." Frankie watched as his sister climbed into the mountain of cushions and peered out with just her eyes showing.

"Chloe what's the plan?" Frankie asked as he turned to his friend.

"Me? What makes you think I have a plan?" Chloe asked.

"Come on, we both know you have a million ways to capture this alien queen. What's the best way?" Frankie demanded.

"Fine. We need to get her in the living room. We need to set traps to encourage her that way." Chloe said as she looked at Frankie, happy that he trusted her.

"I'll help set traps." Kevin said.

"Great, and Marko, where is he?" Chloe looked around and then jumped as the door to the garage opened.

"The sleigh is safe inside, although I don't know if the reindeer will stay out of the boxes of Christmas decorations." Marko said as he came inside. "They are already eating the fake trees. What else should I do?"

"We need a command station, take everyone's phones and place them all around the house. I will connect to them and we can see what is happening." Chloe instructed.

"CCTV. Understood!" Marko said as he collected everyone's phone and started to look for places to put them.

"We have a box of old phones you could use." Frankie suggested as he reached into a cupboard and brought out a large box of old gadgets.

"That's great. You and Marko get on with it." Chloe urged.

"What do you want me to do?" Sophia asked.

"Tracking." Chloe answered quickly. "Here, take my phone and keep us updated on the queens progress. We need to know when that ship is going to be here."

"I'm on it." Sophia said as she took the phone and went to join Jess in the sofa fort.

Chloe turned to Kevin who had emptied his satchel of all the different tools that could be used, fishing wire, slime and Lego were all options on the table in front of her.

"Let's see what we can make." Chloe said as she looked at the tools in front of her.

"I thought you were brave to let the aliens chase you in the mall." Marko told Frankie as they started to place the camera phones around the house.

"Thanks. You still haven't told me what happened at Disney World. How did you create living cartoons?" Frankie asked.

"We found this pen in Walt Disney's secret room. Sophia drew animals and they came alive." Marko started to explain.

"Several alien ships are heading this way." Sophia said suddenly. "We are going to be outnumbered. This won't be enough."

"What do you suggest?" Her brother asked as he reached up and placed a camera on a bookcase.

"We have to stop any aliens from getting inside. Only the queen can be allowed in." Sophia explained.

"I know, but how do you plan on stopping them?" Chloe asked as she set up some dominoes, careful not to knock them over.

"I have an idea, but I need to borrow Kevin." Sophia said as she gave Chloe her phone back.

"Okay then, good luck!" Chloe agreed.

"What? Don't I get a say in this?" Kevin argued.

"Nope, now come on." Sophia pulled him away through the garage door as he looked back in protest.

"Wait." Marko shouted. Kevin's face lit up as he thought Marko was about to volunteer to take his place outside, where the aliens were. "Take these with you and set them up outside."

Marko threw a couple of old phones at Kevin who caught them in each hand.

"Good idea." Sophia agreed. "I'll be in contact if we need anything."

The door closed behind them and the house was quiet again.

"Jess, are you okay in there?" Frankie asked as he walked past his sisters hidden location.

"I'm fine." She replied.

"Great. In a few moments we are going to join you in there so make some room." Frankie explained.

"Here, take this." Chloe passed a phone through the peephole. "When that little dot gets close let us know."

"Will do!" Jess said, suddenly happy that she had a role to play.

The house was starting to look ready and Chloe stood up admiring her creation.

"Do you think it will work?" Frankie asked.

"It better. Just one last thing." Chloe ran across to the kitchen where she had left something filling with water in the sink.

"They are nearly here." Jess shouted.

"Right. Places everybody." Marko said as he made his way carefully up the stairs. "Good luck!"

"Shouldn't we check up on Sophia and Kevin?" Frankie asked as he followed Chloe into the sofa fort.

"Already done. They are in position outside. Just one last thing to do."

Chloe took her phone from Jess and tapped on the screen a few times until the lights in the house turned off.

"When did you get access to the lights?" Frankie asked.

"Come on, I have been coming to your house for years, of course I have access to all your lights, TV's and computers." Chloe jested. "Now it's time to watch and wait."

For the first time that night the house was dark and silent. Chloe tapped another app that allowed her to see all the cameras that were placed around the house and outside.

The street was deadly quiet and there was no sign of Sophia or Kevin. Then the video feed changed as several spaceships hovered over the house before lowering and landing in the street. It was time.

Chapter 24

"I can't believe you haven't seen Home Alone. Everything we are doing now, it's basically the entire movie!" Frankie said to Chloe as she sat huddled around the small screen inside Jess's fort.

Outside three spaceships had landed. They were huge. Much bigger than any Frankie had seen, and they struggled to fit in the cosy, little street. Their legs quietly crushing the freshly fallen snow in the neighbour's gardens. Next doors prized flower bed had been crushed.

Ramps unfolded from the middle of these huge ships and dozens of little green men appeared holding their devices. They were ready for a battle.

The street was quiet, everything was still, even the birds weren't awake yet. The aliens were being careful, slowly sneaking up on the house, ready to pounce.

As they approached, they moved together, and as a group they all jumped in fear as the house came alive. Christmas music rang out and the entire house flashed with hundreds of Christmas lights, taking everyone by surprise.

"I guess Sophia found a use for your old Christmas decorations." Chloe joked as she watched the street outside light up in a colourful display.

"It's so bright!" Jess said as she peeked out of the window in the fort. The lights were so bright they could be seen through the curtains, causing shadows to dance around the living room.

The aliens blinded by the light and scared by the Christmas music took a step back. They were not prepared for this, they thought they were sneaking up on Jess, not walking into a trap. They looked around, urging each other on, but none of them moved. It was at this moment, when the aliens were most confused that the lawn sprinklers came on. The little jets of water were no longer facing the lawn, but instead pointed out into the street, directly at the aliens.

"She has moved the sprinklers too!" Frankie commented. "Dad spent ages setting them up, more time than it would have taken just to water the lawn!"

The water hit the little aliens square in the face and given that it was the middle of December, it was very cold. So cold that the little aliens green skin started to turn blue.

Some of them ran, others were hit with such force that they were knocked over. The water started to quickly freeze as it landed on the snow-covered ground, and when the aliens turned to run they slipped, toppled over and struggled to get up without sliding around more. It was like watching baby giraffes on ice, these aliens had no co-ordination and were pushing each other over as they tried to climb to their feet.

Eventually the sprinklers stopped, but the aliens found their boots frozen to ice puddles, unable to move. Some were bent over, others were lying down. Any part of them that was touching the ground, was now frozen to it.

Aliens started to appear from the other two spaceships but soon stopped to witness this disaster. At first, they laughed, but now that their friends were frozen to the spot they were careful to avoid the water jets.

At least ten aliens had been caught in the ice and were now struggling to get free. There were nearly thirty aliens still trying to figure out a safe way into the house.

Of course, Sophia and Kevin still had a few tricks left. The two of them appeared out of the bushes and opened the garage door. Eight reindeer ran out, their heads down moving towards the crowd of aliens in the street. Moments later the reindeer were having a blast, smashing their antlers into the aliens and popping them into balls of slime every time.

The aliens started to aim their devices at the huge beasts but once again they were too slow. By the time they had taken aim and pressed the button, the reindeer were gone, already attacking a new target.

"What was that?" Chloe asked as she tapped on one of the cameras near the front door. "I am sure I saw something.

The camera was focused on the porch, with bushes lining the path. Then the aliens came into sight. A group of eight moved slowly towards the front door. Sophia and Kevin hadn't noticed them, and they were close.

"They are coming in." Chloe radioed to Marko upstairs. "Eight of them through the front door."

The handle twisted and slowly the door opened with a creak. An alien head appeared in the gap to make sure the way was clear. The house was dark, except for the occasional Christmas light outside that lit up and chased shadows around the room.

The porch and the stairwell appeared empty, just as Chloe had planned, and the aliens grew in confidence, opening the door and walking in. As the last one entered, Frankie pulled on the fishing wire that he had tied to the door, ran through the house and back, into the fort. The door slammed shut behind them with a loud bang, then silence.

The noise startled the group that huddled at the bottom of the stairs. They were on edge, scared, and couldn't figure out what to do next. Then a single slinky started to make its way down the staircase, one creepy step at a time.

The aliens were so interested at the little spring slowly falling down the stairs that they didn't notice the giant gift-wrapped boxes flying straight for them from above.

Marko knew these aliens could not be destroyed, the military had already tried bigger weapons and had no success. It took magic, and Santa was not around to make magical items.

There was a sleigh in the garage. And while Marko was parking it, he found it packed full of magical items including large rolls of wrapping paper and tinsel. When this empty, gift-wrapped box collided with two of the aliens they exploded into slime as if the box weighed several tons. The remaining six scattered, shocked at their friends who were now splattered around the room.

Two of them ran into the dining room, tripping over a thin wire as they did. They flew across the room and landed in a pile. As they struggled to get up a tapping noise started to surround them.

As they got to their feet they watched as a cascade of dominoes clattered around the room, across the wooden floor and splitting. Some dominoes went up over the table while others fell under the chairs. The whole point was to get the aliens to look at the window, and as the dominoes fell, the aliens turned and watched as the little blocks came to an end in a fancy display underneath the large window.

They didn't see the large red blanket with white fur edges fall from the ceiling, trapping them underneath. They struggled at first, fighting for freedom. The shapes of two aliens underneath started to slow, then the giant blanket fell flat on the ground as green smoke escaped from the edges. The aliens were gone.

Two more ran up the stairs but Marko was ready and waiting. He didn't want to give away his position, so he stayed out of sight behind Frankie's bedroom door, watching through the crack. The aliens made it to the top of the stairs, and he pulled on the rope in his hands.

Marko had attached the reins from the sleigh, the same reins that made the reindeer fly, to the bathroom door handle. As he pulled they snapped tight, across the landing and straight into the aliens.

The force from the ropes should have been enough to send the aliens back down the stairs, but instead, these were magical and once again the aliens vanished in a cloud of green mist.

The final two aliens headed towards the living room where Chloe, Frankie and Jess were waiting in the sofa castle.

"On three." Chloe whispered as she watched the screen. Then she gestured one… two… three! Frankie stood up, throwing the cushions everywhere and destroying the little fortress. It didn't matter that he was exposed, he was holding something much more powerful.

The aliens were facing away from the fort, but they soon turned around to see Frankie towering over them, silhouetted by the bright lights from outside as he swung something large and golden in his hand.

It hit both the aliens with one simple swing. A large bell that had hung on the sleigh clanked as it hit the little men. Instantly a cloud of green vapour appeared and flew up the chimney.

"All clear." Chloe said into her phone. A smile grew on her face as she looked at Frankie, holding the bell in his hand.

She reached up and gave him a huge hug.

"Eww! My brother has germs you know!" Jess scowled at the two hugging teenagers.

Moments later Marko came running down the stairs, magical rope in his hands, and he was joined by Kevin and Sophia who stumbled through the door from the garage giggling at the frozen aliens in the street.

"Outside is clear!" Sophia said as she and Kevin ran over to the rest of the group who were now stood next to the fireplace.

"We did it!" Marko yelled.

"Aren't you forgetting something?" A hissing growl came from the shadows in the kitchen.

Everyone stopped, smiles turned to fear as everyone saw what was in front of them. Standing on four legs, with four arms in the air and giant horns on her head, was the Queen.

Chapter 25

"I believe you have something that I want." The Queen hissed as she walked her four-legged body out of the dark kitchen and into the living room.

Fear should have struck them, but they were getting used to saving the world. Frankie knew what to do. Holding the bell up high he took aim and threw it directly at the queen's head.

It flew across the room in slow motion. At least that was how Frankie experienced the moment. His heart beating in his chest, his chest breathing deeply. He watched as the bell made its way towards the queen. In the back of his mind he could sense his sister hiding in the pile of cushions under the sofa.

The golden bell clanged as it moved, the lights from outside flashed on and off and everyone held their breath. The bell was on target to hit the queen. Then a green hand grabbed it, catching it in mid-air, scrunched it up like it was made of paper and threw it to the ground.

Frankie froze. That was a metal, magical bell, that had destroyed aliens the moment it touched them. The queen treated it like a piece of rubbish.

Marko didn't have time to react. He was already throwing his magic rope, ready to see her pop into slime just like the other aliens. Instead, the queen caught the rope and pulled.

Marko was jerked across the room and into the queens waiting arms. She quickly wrapped him up in the rope and dropped him to the ground. He couldn't move, he could barely breathe. It all happened so quickly, one moment he was standing, the next he was wriggling on the floor trying to untie himself.

"That's impossible!" Marko stuttered, using all his energy to force the words out.

"Your pathetic magical items don't work on me, you foolish creatures! Now tell me, where is the key!" The queen yelled, dripping, and spitting slime all over Sophia who was now the closest.

"We aren't going to tell you!" Kevin said as he stepped in between the queen and Sophia. The queen towered over him as she leaned back on her hind legs.

"Get out of my way!" She yelled as she cast him aside with one swipe of her arms, throwing him into the wall opposite. Kevin's body slumped on the floor and he didn't move.

"What have you done with Santa?" Sophia asked.

"Your precious Santa Claus, he was a weak protector. When you join me, you'll see what a true leader looks like!" The queen hissed as she approached Sophia, noticing the dried slime all over her. "You seem to have the guts of my army all over you. How many have you killed? I could use a warrior like you."

"I would never join you." Sophia whispered as the queen lifted her in the air.

"Very well. Then you will suffer the same fate as everyone else." The queen threw Sophia down towards Kevin.

He reached out to catch his friend, breaking her fall. She sat there trying to get back to her feet, she was not done yet.

The queen started coughing and spat out a slimeball that flew across the room and landed on Sophia's legs, pinning her down and sticking her to the floor.

"If Santa didn't tell you we were here, then how did you know?" Chloe asked as she stood up straight to the alien menace.

"Your friend. He let the secret out when you were all trapped in that mall." The queen said as she held up a device and pressed a button. A recording of Frankie's voice played.

"My sister is out there with the key and I need to protect her!" His voice echoed around the living room.

"After my army heard that, I didn't need that fat man anymore, so I disposed of him. He cannot fly as well as his reindeer." The queen laughed as she moved passed Chloe and straight to Frankie. "Your sister has the key. Where is she?"

The queen moved towards Frankie and reached out to grab him, to lift him up. But Frankie held strong, his hand met hers and pushed it away.

"I am not going to tell you! You will never find her!" Frankie said as he stood up straight, trying to match the alien's height as he looked her in the eyes.

"I don't believe you!" The queen snarled as she put her face up against his. "If you tell me, you and your sister will be unharmed I promise."

"Don't listen to her!" Chloe shouted. "She has killed Santa! She can't be trusted!"

The queen kicked out a leg. It hit Chloe in her chest, throwing her back and through the air. She landed on the far side of the room next to Marko. He was busy gasping for air as his rope prison made it difficult to breathe. She started to untie him and collapsed again, realising that she was in more pain than she thought.

"Tell me where you're hiding the key!" The queen hissed one more time, staring straight into Frankie's eyes.

"I will never tell you!" Frankie said with confidence. He believed his own words, there was no way he was going to tell the queen that his sister was hiding underneath the piles of pillows. She would have to search the entire world first. Unfortunately, his eyes didn't have the same idea.

Briefly he glanced at the sofa, at where Jess was hiding, and this was all it took. The queen noticed, smiled, and tossed him aside. She marched over to the sofa, pulling away the pillows and revealing the little girl whose eyes started to flood.

"No!" Frankie shouted as he moved forward once again to attack the queen, but it was too late.

"There you are!" The queen said.

Jess lay on the ground, holding the clover up like a protective shield.

"One more key, one more planet to increase my power! One more item to fight my enemies with!" The queen reached out to grab it. Jess opened her eyes to see the grin on the evil creature's face. Her long teeth showing through green lips and determination in her eyes.

She was about to scream, to yell in fear, and she closed her eyes, waiting for the attack. An attack that never came.

Looking at the queen again she noticed the determination had turned to sadness and confusion, and then to pain. The queen stumbled, away from Jess.

Her four arms were clawing at something on her back, something she couldn't reach.

"You're on my naughty list!" Santa said from the fireplace. In his hand he held another piece of coal and he slammed it into the queen's chest.

The large alien started to glow. She moved around violently trying to get rid of the charcoal that was stuck on her skin. She lit up the room in a bright light that made everyone hide their eyes, then she turned to smoke as lumps of coal fell to the floor.

"Santa!" Jess flew across the room and grabbed him by the waist, hugging him just like last night.

"Well done everybody!" Santa turned to the group of teenagers who were scattered around the room.

"Can someone help me please?" Sophia asked as she was still stuck to the floor with the horrible green goo.

"Of course." Santa bent over and touched a piece of coal to the slime. It quickly turned to liquid and Sophia could move her legs again.

"Charcoal, the best cleanser around!" Sophia commented. "I really need some for Christmas!"

"Oh boy!" Marko said sarcastically as Chloe finished untying him.

"Santa! We thought she killed you." Frankie said.

"She had me on board her ship, I was trapped, and my magic wouldn't work. Every time she tried to get information out of me, I just laughed 'Ho. Ho. Ho.'" Santa explained as he bellowed his famous laugh which made everyone else smile. "Then, she played me a recording, of you saying you need to protect your sister. She no longer needed me, so she threw me out of her spacecraft, but she didn't know I had one reindeer waiting for me. Rudolf! He isn't the fastest which is why I am a bit late getting here."

"I think you got here just in time!" Chloe remarked.

"It's a good job you held out as long as you did, with all these crazy traps. You sure did make a mess." Santa said looking around at the destruction in the house.

"My mum is going to kill us!" Frankie said, also noticing the mess for the first time and snapping back to reality.

"I can't allow Earth's saviours to get in trouble." Santa chuckled as he reached into his sack and pulled out an elf. "This is Bob. He cleans my workshop. I think you know what to do."

The little elf turned into a blur of activity as he zoomed around the house cleaning up and returning everything to normal. The dominoes went back, the slime was tidied up, the sofa castle was torn down. A few seconds later he was finished and Frankie had never seen the living room look so clean.

"Thank you. How can we ever repay you?" Jess asked.

"Repay me? You saved the world, all of you!" Santa said, holding his hands out. "Whenever someone does a good deed, treats someone else with kindness or makes someone else feel good about themselves, that's what gives me my power, and right now the world is happy!"

The little elf, Bob, started to tug on Santa's jacket as he pointed to his watch.

"Is it that time already? I must go, I have a busy day coming up, but stay good, and be kind to each other!" The big, red, jolly man and his little elf turned to smoke and disappeared up the chimney leaving everyone in the room looking around in amazement.

The room was quiet again. Then the door handle to the garage started to twist. Slowly the door opened with a creek, everyone jumped and turned around, ready to attack whatever was trying to sneak up on them.

"Sorry, but would you mind giving me a hand getting my sleigh out of the garage?" Santa asked as he popped his head around the door. "And has anyone seen my reindeer?"

"We'll help!" Marko said as he jumped up and dragged Kevin and Sophia with him.

"I'm coming, no need to pull me!" Sophia moaned as they left the room, leaving Frankie and Chloe behind.

"Well, you saved the world, what are you going to do now?" Chloe asked.

"*We* saved the world." Frankie corrected her. "I think *we* deserve a break."

Chapter 26

The house was quiet. Everyone was earning some much-needed sleep when Frankie's mum came downstairs with the little dog following her.

"Wake up everybody! The aliens have gone!" Mrs Thomson shouted as she walked into the living room, stepping over the kids to turn the TV on.

"I had the strangest dream!" Frankie said as he sat up briefly, then Dexter landed on his face and started to lick him, forcing him back onto the floor.

"It's on the news, the aliens have disappeared." His mum said excitedly. "Wake up everybody. I told you everything would be fine in the morning."

The room stirred as everybody moaned.

"What time is it?" Sophia asked as she turned over.

"What on Earth!" Frankie's mum gasped when she saw Sophia. "I don't know what you were doing last night but you're going to go mental when you see yourself."

"I can explain." Sophia said as she reached to cover up her face. The last time she checked she was covered in dust and dead alien slime. Mrs Thomson held out her phone showing the selfie camera.

"It was…" Sophia started but then caught herself in the camera. The slime was gone, the dust was not there, she was clean again, somehow, but her face was covered in drawings of moustaches and doodles.

Marko and Kevin started to laugh in the corner.

"Sorry Sophia." Kevin snorted.

"Oh well, it could be worse." Sophia shrugged off the comments, much to the amazement of Mrs Thomson.

"Are you feeling okay Sophia?" Frankie's mum asked.

"Never better." Sophia said calmly.

"Okay then." Mrs Thomson replied. "Frankie will you open the curtains?"

He got up and started to open the thick curtains at the front of the house. The sunlight hit him, blinding him but also warming him. Then he heard the news report behind him on the TV.

"We are getting new video from the events in Las Vegas." The news reporter started. "Santa and a young boy can be seen leaving the Luxor hotel and boarding his sleigh."

Frankie froze. He knew what was coming.

"Frankie? Why are you on TV? What did you lot get up to last night?" His mum asked as she watched a closeup of Frankie's face on the screen.

"Mum, you wouldn't believe it even if I told you." Frankie replied as he opened the curtains revealing three large spaceships outside the house and a dozen aliens that were still frozen to the ground.

Mrs Thomson fainted.

"Well done, you killed her!" Chloe joked as she pulled Frankie's mum onto a chair.

"I think we all need to get our stories straight." Frankie started to explain, but then his eyes were caught by the screen again.

"Last night it seems these five teenagers went on a worldwide adventure with Santa to save the world.

Wherever you are now, we thank you." The news lady said as a picture came on the screen of the five of them holding their weapons inside the Mall of America.

"Actually, that's a good picture of us all, makes us look like superheroes." Marko commented. "And I doubt we can keep this a secret, if that was your plan?"

"I suppose your right." Frankie agreed.

"We are getting reports of strange activity in Florida, James Turner is on the scene for us." The news screen changed and a giant cartoon dragon appeared, sitting on top of the castle in the Disney park. Frankie could just about make out some other cartoons in the background, they were on the rollercoasters and enjoying themselves in the gift shops. Then the screen went off.

"Perhaps we should explain what happened at Disney before you learn about it on the news." Marko said.

EPILOGUE

"There is only five minutes until midnight!" Chloe said as she poured a glass of orange juice for Sophia and herself.

"And he still hasn't asked you to kiss him?" Sophia asked.

"Nope, not yet." She confirmed.

"I'll figure out why!" Sophia said, storming off towards the group of boys in the far corner of the room.

The night had been great so far. It was Frankie's idea to hold a house party for New Years Eve, and everyone was invited. The house was full, neighbours, family and anyone who wanted to meet Frankie and the gang who had saved the world. Of course, he only wanted to spend New Year's Eve with one person. He hadn't even seen Chloe since the night of the aliens.

"What are you doing?" Sophia asked as she stamped over. "This is your first New Year's party with Chloe, get over there! Get ready to kiss her!" She ordered Frankie, pulling him out of his seat and throwing him across the room in Chloe's general direction before quickly taking his seat so he couldn't return.

"So, what did Santa get you for Christmas?" Kevin asked.

"Why do you ask?" Sophia tried to deflect the conversation.

"No reason, it's just that Marko told us about the trainers he received that apparently make him incredible at sports."

"Ahem." Marko coughed.

"Sorry, *more* incredible at sports. I was just wondering if you got anything special?" Kevin asked again. "Did you get that charcoal gift set you wanted?"

"Well I did get a gift set. But it was a bit lousy to be honest." Sophia said as she watched Kevin's smile fade. "Full of cheap stuff, but it was from Marko so what should I expect!"

"Oh, right, did you get anything else?" Kevin asked one more time.

"You first. Did you get anything from Santa?"

"Well…" He pulled out a piece of paper that had a map of the world on it. "Here, hold my hand."

Carefully Sophia held his hand as he pointed at the map, hovering over France. The room around them shook and shimmered, then the two of them were sat at the top of the Eifel Tower, overlooking Paris.

"Wow!" Sophia said as she looked around the city. "Paris at New Years, you sure know how to impress a girl!"

"We aren't really here." Kevin reached out and touched the city, causing it to ripple just in front of them. "The map is like a camera, it lets me visit anywhere in the world, but I cannot change anything!"

"This is awesome! And I loved your present! Thank you!" Sophia said as she squeezed his hand and smiled back at him.

Kevin couldn't help but grin from ear to ear. He took his hand off the map and the world returned, they were sitting back in Frankie's living room again, still holding hands.

"You know you pull the strangest faces when you do that." Marko said as he sat opposite them and watched.

"You really like the gift set I got you?" Kevin asked, still blushing.

"Yeah, it goes well with my present from Santa."

"What was that?" Kevin asked.

"She got a necklace that lets her see anyone's true desire." Marko interrupted.

"Really? You can tell what they want the most?" Kevin asked.

"Santa wants me to help people realise their dreams." Sophia explained. "Let me try it on you."

Kevin backed away and went red in the face.

"I don't think so." He said, holding up his hands.

"Come on, Marko let me do it on him, I saw him holding some trophy."

"It was the World Cup and yeah, who doesn't dream of leading your country to the final?" Marko sniffed.

"Fine." Kevin lowered his hands and allowed Sophia to put the necklace around his neck. She opened the locket at the front and watched for a few moments. "Well?"

"It's as I thought." Sophia said. "I don't blame you for wanting that, and who knows, you might actually get it."

"Get what? What did you see?" Kevin asked impatiently, trying to look down at the locket under his chin.

"Unfortunately, if I told you it wouldn't come true." Sophia said as she smiled back at him.

"The story of my life." Kevin said as he reached for his drink. "What do you think about those two?"

Frankie covered the distance between him and Chloe at the slowest speed known to man. If you weren't watching him, you would swear he was standing still.

"Why is he so nervous? He has been friends with Chloe for years. Just because they go on a magical adventure and he saves her life, why should that change anything?" Marko asked.

"Hi." Frankie said nervously. "We were just talking about what Santa gave us for Christmas, I assume he left you something?" Frankie asked as he approached Chloe. She wore a long dress and was looking very fancy, as was everybody.

"Yeah, you know what he gave me." Chloe replied. "Do I?"

"I got that guitar at the mall." She reminded him.

"Oh yeah. A thunderbird?" Frankie tried to remember.

"A Gibson Firebird, but close enough. It sounds awesome and just holding it gives me inspiration for all kinds of songs. I've already written one album." Chloe explained. "What about you?"

Frankie held out his hand and displayed a new watch. It didn't look like anything special, it had buttons and a date indicator, but otherwise it just looked like a nice, expensive watch.

"Cool, what does it do?" Chloe asked.

"It tells the time. What do you think a watch does?" He joked.

"Oh, okay. I only ask because I am sure my guitar is magical." Chloe said as everybody around him started to call out 'FIVE!

"Well... there is more to my watch. Hold my hand and I'll show you." Frankie said, holding out his hands.

Without hesitation Chloe grabbed them and squeezed tight. Once again, the crowd around them called out…
'FOUR!'

"I can make the whole world slow down." Frankie said as he pressed the watch and the crowd around slowed, their movement's becoming half as fast, then a quarter, then they seemed to be stopped still.

"Wow!" Chloe said, getting up and looking at the crowd as they moved in slow motion. "This is pretty cool. Just imagine the things you could get done with all the time in the world."

"It's useful, sure, but it gets pretty boring, having all this time and no-one to share it with." Frankie said as he pressed on the watch again and the world returned to normal just in time to hear the crowd shout 'ONE! Happy New Year!"

Fireworks exploded in the street but Frankie could no longer see anything. He was too busy kissing Chloe.

"Get off me!" Sophia yelled as she threw Kevin to the floor.

"I thought I might take a chance, be romantic and spontaneous." Kevin replied.

"Dude, that's my sister!" Marko showed his disgust at seeing his friend trying to kiss his sister.

"I'm sorry." Kevin held his head in shame.

"I didn't mean stop, I meant get off me, if we are going to do this, let's do it right." Sophia said as she stood up and pulled Kevin to his feet before the kissing resumed.

"Great!" Marko said, looking around for something to distract him. Everyone around him was kissing each other. At his feet was Dexter, wagging his tail and looking happy.

"I'm not kissing you if that's what you're thinking!"

A MESSAGE FROM THE AUTHOR

I hope you have enjoyed this story.

The idea came to me one Christmas as I was watching one of the many "aliens taking over the world" movies and I happened to glance over at a picture of Santa.

'Why don't you help?' I asked.

The rest of that evening I thought about what Santa could do if aliens did invade.

You never know when inspiration for a story is going to hit you. I made notes, came up with ideas and I hope you have enjoyed the story I have created.

If you liked it then please look out for my other stories. They too are filled with crazy, wild and wacky adventures for people of all ages to read and enjoy!

Merry Christmas!

Printed in Great Britain
by Amazon

67117482R00128